HOLD *me* HARDER

TO HAVE AND TO HOLD SERIES

D1520733

HOLD *me*
HARDER

TO HAVE AND TO HOLD SERIES

RENEE DOMINICK

Entangled Publishing, LLC
2614 South Timberline Road
Suite 105, PMB 159
Fort Collins, CO 80525
Visit our website at www.entangledpublishing.com.

Scorched is an imprint of Entangled Publishing, LLC.

Edited by Brenda Chin
Cover design by Cover Couture
Cover art from iStock and Deposit Photos

Manufactured in the United States of America

First Edition December 2017

entangled
scorched

To those who propped me up when my resolve wavered, and to Romance readers, whose enormous hearts never cease to astound me.

Chapter One

The chain of emails stacked up on Natalie's phone. As fast as her finger flicked across the screen, she couldn't out-scroll the incoming shit hitting the proverbial fan. It was not a good day to be out of the office, but her little sister, Chloe, had insisted on this wedding-party bonding weekend, as if they could all just drop their jobs and their lives and come to middle-of-effing-nowhere Idaho for three days. Worse, the best man—Natalie's ex, Ryan—had managed to squeeze into her limo at the last moment. She caught him watching her more than once, his vivid blue gaze palpable and almost unbearably heavy. It had been weeks since she'd kicked him out of the condo they'd been sharing and she hadn't spoken more than a few words to him since.

When the limo's tires changed from humming across asphalt to crunching over gravel, Natalie muttered a profanity-enhanced sigh of relief.

Her twin brother leaned across her to gawk out the window as they passed the ranch's largest corrals. When their family had vacationed here eight years ago, Rob, the one horse-mad family member, had missed it because of his job.

"Told you," Natalie said, without looking outside. Having been here scores of times, she knew exactly how impressive it all was.

"There's telling me, and then there's seeing for myself." Rob sat back after they passed the barn. "I'd rather have spent the summer here than tutoring athletes in a classroom that smelled like week-old gym socks."

Natalie gave him a sidelong glance. "You say that, but you haven't met Javier," she muttered.

"I'm sure he's no worse than any other horse wrangler," he replied.

"Right." The limo stopped and she looked out the window. The first sight of Javier's lodge never failed to wow her. Gigantic timbers, round and raw, framed a two-story entrance over a sprawling log building. Along the front, a wide, inviting porch extended its full length. Natalie had always thought of it as a Wild West castle made of lodgepole pine. Smaller cabins nestled on the forested hillside behind the main lodge, although the word "cabin" was inadequate. Each was a luxurious little nest.

Here was the scene of her sexual awakening, and Javier, the man responsible, was out there somewhere among the horses. Her eyes darted between the corrals where the Paints and Appaloosas lazed in the afternoon heat, then to the largest of the stables. Odds were, that's where he'd be. Inside, with his sleek Andalusians. She hoped she'd have time to settle in and get over her jitters before she had to face him again after more than a year apart.

Natalie blew out a long breath. A weekend in the presence of two ex-lovers. No wonder she was as nervous as a cat.

The others in her car spilled out like puppies, joining the crowd from the first limo. Most of the bridesmaids had coordinated their attire like the recent sorority refugees they were, dressing in western-style shirts tied at the waist, cowboy boots, tight jeans, and straw cowgirl hats. Natalie, on the other hand, had spent her morning at work. She arrived in a gray pin-striped skirt, silk shirt, and high-heeled pumps just barely on the businesslike end of the scale.

The third limo pulled up just as Natalie was stepping out, and the other girls raised a cloud of dust as they danced over to welcome the bride and groom to be.

"Yee-HAW!" Chloe shouted, waving her hat overhead as she emerged from her limo, with Dave, her impending husband, right behind. He grabbed her hips and they gyrated together, a grinding Texas two-step.

Natalie rolled her eyes and leaned against the side of the limo while the driver unloaded the suitcases, her finger scrolling the message queue, the phone vibrating nonstop in her hand. Her boss thrived on getting the masses riled, and not one of her idiot coworkers could resist the reply all button. She had the sudden urge to shove the phone into her panties and let it do some actual good. The idea brought a smile to her lips. *Sorry, boss, I couldn't respond. The phone was otherwise engaged.*

"What's so funny?"

Ryan stood too close for comfort. She frowned at him. "Nothing."

He tugged on her tote bag. "Lime green? Taking a walk on the wild side, Nat?" He tilted his head at an oblique angle, his crooked, disarming smile inviting her to smile back. Before, she would have. Not today.

"Yes, that's what me carrying a lime green bag means," she said, dropping her phone inside it.

His smile faded and he shook his head. "C'mon, Nat. We're going to be in each other's company a lot this weekend. Can't we—?"

"Not if I can help it," she said, cutting him off and

pretending to look for something else in her bag.

"It's been a month." He pushed back an errant lock of hair that had fallen across his face, his long, elegant fingers forking through the sable strands. "Don't you think we should eventually talk?"

Natalie pressed her lips together. She didn't want him trying to penetrate her thoughts, probing for weak spots. There'd been nothing actually wrong between them when she'd run; in fact, their relationship had been adventurous and full of laughs until his taste for sexual adventure trod too close to the lifestyle she'd lived with Javier, the one she'd left here at the ranch. He'd crossed a line she hadn't told him existed, and she'd panicked.

The limo driver dropped her overstuffed Louis Vuitton suitcase on the ground, and Ryan reached for its handle at the same time she did, his fingers brushing hers. "Let me help you."

"I got it," she said, her molars clenched. She didn't want to walk beside him, didn't want him to push her to talk, didn't want him to make her regret. The phone buzzed inside her bag. She grabbed the handle of her suitcase and jerked it away. "I have to go deal with the office."

She turned away from the disappointment in Ryan's gaze, and cursed her heart for breaking just a little more.

The suitcase weighed a ridiculous amount for a weekend getaway, and its inadequate wheels threatened to fly off as she bumped and jostled it over the uneven ground. Between it and her need to tiptoe across the gravel path in stiletto heels, Natalie made slow progress. She was grateful when several of the ranch's young, cowboy-attired employees burst through the front doors of the lodge and fanned out among the arriving guests, greeting them and helping with the luggage. A calloused thumb brushed across the underside of her wrist as someone reached for her bag.

"Natalie," Javier said, his quiet greeting catching her off guard. "I've missed you, *amorcita*."

Damn. His heavy Andalusian accent, warm as the land from which he hailed, twined with the lingering brush of his thumb, and together they welcomed her back. Javier didn't smile when she looked up at him—he'd always been circumspect in the presence of her family—but affection was there in his eyes. He'd changed little since she'd last seen him. His hair remained defiantly dark, as if not even one strand of silver dared appear, his olive-colored eyes, framed by curling black lashes and severe brows, still pierced, and his skin would forever be burnished bronze by hours outdoors.

"I would have said you'd be the next to last person I'd see here again," he teased.

"Yes, well, my mother wasn't invited this weekend." It was an old joke between them. A dude ranch—even a luxury one—had not been her mother's idea of a real vacation. She'd hated it. Vocally.

It hadn't really been Natalie's ideal trip, either, but she had distracted herself by flitting between the young cowhands, until Javier—ten years older than her and miles further on in worldliness—had ejected her from his barns for the duration of their stay. Outside in the corrals, he'd looked down his crooked patrician nose and waved her off with undisguised superiority...and drew her to him like a bee to lavender. She'd fallen at his feet, and he'd introduced her to the world of sensual dominance.

"Obviously, I didn't expect to be back, but I wasn't about to disappoint Chloe," Natalie said, her smile barely a twitch.

"And this has you distressed."

Her gaze slid away from his all-too-observant one. "It's a bad day to be out of the office." Natalie shrugged to mask her unease. "And it's not easy for me to be here. You know that."

Javier scanned the bridal party, nineteen of them

stretched out along the path from the front steps of the lodge to the limousines. His gaze sharpened when his survey swept past her shoulder. "Ah, so this is your Ryan," he said. "You're right. You chose the corporate version of me."

Though Natalie had been determined to stay away from Javier once she turned her back on life as a submissive, their long history made a clean break all but impossible. They kept in touch via the occasional email or phone call.

"He's nothing like you." Notwithstanding the dark hair, broad shoulders, and self-assured manner. Other than that, they weren't alike at all.

Javier clicked his tongue, but the tilt of his brows gave away his amusement. "You're being very hard on him. Are we to inflict some payback this weekend?"

"It wasn't my intention, no," Natalie said, though in the end her intentions wouldn't matter. Javier knew she had run from Ryan and why. Her first distressed phone call had been to him. If he wanted to inflict payback, he would. Still, she said, "I've been successfully ignoring him."

"He's not going to allow it. You know this, right?"

"Allow what, being ignored? He doesn't have a say in it."

Javier gave her an exasperated look, then collapsed the handle of her suitcase and hoisted it onto his shoulder in one smooth movement. "We shall see." He took off at a sedate walk, as if hauling forty bulky pounds on his shoulder was nothing. Which, she supposed, it wasn't, when he could carry a newborn foal or a recalcitrant calf with the same casual ease.

Natalie watched him stride away, as affected by him as she'd been from day one. His backside, encased in jeans so well-worn they molded his shape like a second skin, made her fingers itch to caress the familiar curve of it. She ran her gaze up to his shoulders and over his taut forearms, on full display below the rolled-up cuffs of his shirt. He'd never lacked for physical beauty, but it was his quiet, steady dominance that had attracted her from the start.

As if he felt her looking, he turned back, a shallow cleft between his brows. "Are you coming?"

She hoisted her tote bag onto her shoulder, and the weight of it dragged her blouse askew, exposing the curve of her breast.

Javier's gaze dipped and then rose back to her face, his eyelids lowering as a flash of disappointment crossed his features. Anyone bothering to look would see nothing, but she knew better. He had always insisted she dress with decorum, disapproved of revealing attire—except, of course, when he had decreed it, and it was usually for his eyes only.

Natalie flushed, and her fingers tingled with the sudden influx of blood. She raised a shaky hand and drew the silk back into place. She wasn't his anymore, but his expression implied repercussions nonetheless.

He nodded his approval and turned to make his way to the lodge.

The breath she released was as unsteady as her hand had been. She had left Javier when she could no longer reconcile the two sides of herself: the alpha professional, to whom others looked for guidance and leadership, and the sexual submissive, to whom it sometimes felt that this man had become more necessary than air. Now, two minutes in his presence and it was as if she'd made no choice at all. This had been her fear in coming back, this feeling of being exactly where she belonged.

Ryan drew abreast of her, his speculative gaze moving between her and her retreating suitcase. "So, this is the cowboy."

Natalie scowled at him. Ryan knew she'd had a prior relationship with a rancher, but she wasn't about to confirm his guess.

"Intense guy." He jerked his head toward the lodge. "So, Natalie? Are you coming?" The astute look he gave her spelled trouble. He didn't wait for her answer, just strolled toward the front door, one hand in his pocket, the other towing his black leather carry-on bag behind him.

She tiptoed the final few yards to the front steps of the lodge on unsteady legs. In the lobby, neither her suitcase nor Javier was in sight.

Natalie had chosen to stay in the main lodge rather than share one of the cabins with her sister's friends. When she gave her name at the front desk, the cheery young receptionist handed her a card key and informed her that her bag had already been delivered to her room.

The warm smell of sage welcomed her into the luxury suite, its king-size bed lush with bolsters, pillows, and a down comforter encased in crisp white linens. A brown velveteen chaise sat at an angle next to a picture window, full-length to take advantage of the view of the barns and corrals, and beyond that, the scrubby, pine-covered hills cradling Lake Pend Oreille. Next to the chaise, on a small, round table, sat an enormous bouquet of peonies so deep red they were almost black, sprigs of hibiscus, and stems of fragrant rosemary. Dark and sensual, just like the man who'd gifted them.

She wanted more than anything to sprawl onto the chaise and relax in the sumptuous room. Instead, she set up her laptop and plugged in her overburdened phone to charge. When she found herself staring outside again, she yanked the sheer inner-curtains closed, to at least obscure her view. No time for daydreaming. If she didn't make an appearance on the email chain soon, her boss would pop an artery. Based on her phone-scrolling, this marketing miscue wasn't great, but it wasn't earthshaking—or time-critical—either. It was three a.m. in Shanghai. Since she'd become the company's unofficial crisis manager, she'd had to learn to separate incidents into DEFCON categories, and this one was a low-two, max.

While the computer booted up, she went to her suitcase, kicked off her shoes, and tossed the contents of the bag, looking for more comfortable clothes. Three quiet beeps from the card key mechanism caught her ear. Only one other person would access her room. She turned her head as the door handle lowered.

"*Dios mio*," Javier said, striding inside, the door closing behind him with a solid *click*. He took hold of her hips from behind and pulled her against him, his lips and teeth sweeping down her neck, marking her, claiming her as he'd always done. He wrapped her in familiar scents: ponderosa pine and horse and the tang of the tobacco sticks he chewed while he rode, at once piquant and musky. "I wondered if I would ever get to lay my hands on you again."

She relaxed against him and reached back to slip her hands into his rear pockets.

"How easily she settles back into her native state," he murmured, his lips against her temple.

"Old habits," Natalie said with a quiet laugh.

"It feels good to have you here, *cariño*." His palms drew over the contours of her breasts, down her belly, and out to the sides of her hips.

Even through layers of clothing, her body came alive, her nerves crackling and desperate for a more intimate touch. Skin to skin. The hundreds of days since they'd last been together trailed away like so much dandelion fluff.

"Now tell me the truth," he said, propping his chin on her shoulder. "How have you been?"

She turned in his arms. "I'm fine," she said, touching

her finger to one of the grooves bracketing his mouth and tracing it down to his beard. "You look like an austere Spanish gentleman again." The last time she had come to the ranch, he had just returned from a month-long cattle drive with his whiskers a brillo of unruly tufts that reached for his cheekbones. Now it was trimmed close, its outline sharp.

He brought her fingers to his mouth and bit down on the tips. "He isn't done with you, your Ryan."

Natalie didn't want to discuss Ryan, but she knew Javier wouldn't drop it unless he was satisfied with her answers. She kissed his chin. "He had his chance."

"That isn't what I mean, *cariño*. He wants you. Like this." Javier ran his hands over her bottom. "To be his *pequeña*. His little one."

Natalie shook her head. "He's not—"

Javier put his thumb across her lips. "He is, and he knows what you are. Inside. What you could be with him. Why do you think he brought a submissive to you, if not to invite you to explore?"

She stilled and looked up. "What do you know of him, Javier?"

"What I see with my own eyes, *cariño*."

She stared past his arm. "It doesn't matter. I'm not going back to this life. Not with him." She tried to step out of Javier's arms.

"Stop, *pequeña*," he ordered. His fingers bit into her flesh as he tightened his grip on her bottom. In their everyday conversation, she was *cariño*, sweetheart, but in dominant mode, Javier called her *pequeña*, his little one, the name that demanded her submission.

He ran a finger over her brow and held her wary gaze with his serious one. "I failed you, Natalie. I never taught you to recognize the signs of someone looking for a submissive partner, how to know whether he is the right man for you."

Javier reached behind her head and removed the two wooden picks from her hair, letting it cascade across her shoulders. "I never thought you wouldn't be mine."

Indeed, Javier had molded her from the beginning. Submission had been contrary to everything she thought she valued, and yet, when she gave her cares—and her care—to Javier, her world had changed. She wanted to please him, ached for his guidance, his rewards, and even his punishments. Until the incongruity of her life had begun to prey on her.

"I don't need to recognize signs, *mi sol*. I'm not looking."

He clicked his tongue, a sharp sound so full of disappointment it gave her a frisson of unease. "When did you become silly, Natalie?"

"I'm not silly," she said, bruised by his words. "I wanted to find my own way. And I have."

"Have you? I see your computer and your phone and your corporate clothes." He gestured around the room. "You're the *jefe* there, but what of your other side? You are only half a person right now."

That he so blithely identified her unease made her breath hitch. "More than half," she argued, but she experienced a flutter of anticipation as he moved to sit on the end of the bed.

"Come here, *pequeña*." He waved her over. "Take off my shirt."

Natalie wavered, ready to bolt. Forward or back, she couldn't say, until she took the first step toward him and everything inside her relaxed like a bird settling to roost.

"You knew you couldn't come here and have it any other way between us, right, *cariño*?" he said with a wistful smile.

"I should have." She thought she'd prepared for this trip, mentally. It was disappointing to see how badly she'd fooled herself. She had lived with Javier's control for too long not to fall right back under his influence, especially since she now understood how much she had missed this blanket of tranquility, of not having to choose, of having no choices to make at all.

Her fingers trembled as she fought with the buttons on his shirt, but she finally managed them and pushed the edges aside. As ever, she was undone by the sight of his body, muscled and scarred, marked by a lifetime of working with horses. The bulges of his shoulders and the lines and undulating strata of his chest and abdomen drew her fingertips like a magnet. She reacquainted herself with his body, flicked her nails across his drawn nipples, small but positive proof of how she affected him. Her eyes followed the line of dark hair leading down his abdomen and rested on the ridge evident inside his jeans.

Natalie licked her lips.

He threaded his fingers in her hair and tipped her head back. "I should make you," he said, "but it would be selfish of me." He cupped her breast, drew his thumb back and forth across her nipple, raising it to take between his teeth through her blouse. His hands skimmed down her back, around her hips, and lower, to catch the hem of her skirt on the webs of his thumbs. Dragging upward, he exposed the length of her thighs, her satin and lace underwear, the pale skin of her belly. She stood motionless before him as he slid his thumb up and down the silky front of her panties, the rough edges of a callous snagging the weave.

He pressed his lips to her belly button, coiled his tongue in languid turns from the rim into its basin before moving outward to press kisses around the small bulge of her tummy. Down and down he moved, one kiss at a time, while his fingers smoothed over her bottom and inched under the high arc of lace. His palms settled over her bottom, his fingertips curving into the crack. "You can breathe if you want, *cariño*," he said quietly.

She really couldn't. Breathe. She swayed forward and reached for his shoulder when he drew the front of her underwear aside and touched his tongue to her, following the seam upward, coiling again, this time around the sensitive bud concealed near its apex. She drew in a stuttering breath then, and heard his hum of satisfaction.

He kissed deep in the join of her thigh, nipping the tendon, drawing his tongue through the soft depression inside of her hip bone, and all the while his hands worked on her blouse, unbuttoning it more deftly than she had managed with his shirt. He pushed the silk over her shoulders and drew the backs of his fingers over the flimsy netting of her bra, soothed and pulled at her nipples beneath before leaving her breasts to run a deliciously coarse finger through her folds. He found her wet and wanting. "Come here, *pequeña*," he said, and turned her to sit between his legs, her back to his chest.

When she had settled, he drew a bandana from his pocket and used her thigh like a table to fold it into a neat band. The simple, methodical act delivered a keen ache, no less than any explicit touch he could have teased her with.

With slow, deliberate movements, he smoothed back her hair and covered her eyes with the cloth. Then he sat, still and silent, as he waited for her other senses to engage. This aspect of his dominance had been a surprise to her from the beginning, the rising desperation for his touch she found almost more painful than any physical punishment he might employ as he drew the moment beyond its breaking point.

Finally, Natalie remembered to find the warmth of his hands hovering over her legs, her breasts, to listen to the rhythm of his quieter, calmer breathing. Only then did she relax. And only then did he ease her thighs apart and slip his fingers through flesh ready and waiting, curling and uncurling his fingers over her damp softness. Spirals of sensation unwound within her, careened up her spine and down her legs.

Natalie's head dropped back onto his shoulder and a

moan, part agony, part joy, struggled up her throat.

"How I've missed that sound," Javier said, his thumb circling, his fingers pressing, pulling a soft gasp from her.

He overwhelmed her with sensations inside and out until she was reaching, her fingers digging into his thighs, desperate for release. But, by his rule, she was unable to beg. He would break her in his own time, or not at all.

She had forgotten what it was like to be driven to the edge by his softly spoken erotic praise. To be kept balanced at the tipping point for so long, the pain of it, and the pulses of heat scorching her. The mindfuck of it all. Her breathing was shallow when she breathed at all, for the sound of his voice paralyzed her with hope.

He took her earlobe between his teeth and said, "Look, *mi pequeña.*" He drew off the bandana. "Do you think he's enjoying it?"

Natalie blinked to clear her vision and inhaled a sharp exclamation at what she saw through the filmy curtains. Ryan's familiar outline, standing on the porch outside her room, still as a cardboard silhouette. Lust, hot and demanding, swamped her, made her pulse inside.

"It pleases you," Javier said, his unfaltering fingers winding her to the limit of what she could withstand. She couldn't hold back her mewl of need as she strained between his thighs, her hips tilted into his hand.

"Come for us, then, *pequeña.* Now." His demand, his thumb on her clitoris, his fingers deep inside her, Ryan's presence...all of it sent her soaring, keening into the exquisite darkness.

He held her steady and quiet after, until her mind cleared and her limbs came to solidity again. "How long has he been there?" she groaned.

"Long enough."

Natalie turned her head at an acute angle to glare at him.

"Why would you do that?"

He chuckled, a low rumble against her back. "I only invited him to relax on the chairs out front, to enjoy the vista of the lake and the horses. I doubt he can see inside, *cariño*. His view in is worse than ours out. He's probably trying to figure out if there is a raccoon giving birth under the porch."

She thumped her shoulder blades against his chest. "Beast."

He laughed louder this time, deep and rich and exceedingly rare. The sound made a different sort of warmth blossom through her. Affection, mixed uncomfortably with second thoughts about having tossed this all away.

God, she was pathetic. So easy, so malleable. Twenty minutes and a primal orgasm and she was his again. Her gaze traveled back to the window. She was something much, much darker, too. The voyeuristic thrill of seeing Ryan there, of providing a show, had electrified her.

"He could be your protector, *cariño*. If it can't be me," Javier said, as if he had sensed her thoughts. "And if you wish it."

Natalie looked back at him again, finding his gaze gentle as he stroked the length of her hair. "I don't."

"He can't keep his eyes off you, and with so many miles between us, I can't keep mine *on* you. He took a misstep, but I would mentor him, if you want. Teach him, so that you could have this again."

"I…" She shook her head. "I don't want it again."

His expression turned grim. "I think you do. Only I think you're too stubborn to admit you have been living a lie." Javier eased her to her feet and stood to twitch the heavy velveteen curtains over the sheers. He unbuckled his belt as he stalked back toward the bed. "Give me your hands, *mi pequeña*," he said, the leather snapping through his belt loops. "We're not done here, yet."

Natalie had no idea how much time had passed, only that she ached pleasantly in several places, and her bottom held the shimmering warmth of Javier's handprint. He had already gotten partially dressed, but she still lay facedown on the bed, reveling in his tenderness as he drew the backs of his fingers along her skin from neck to knees. "You're out of practice, *cariño*, but not so far as I thought you must be."

His praise swirled through her like a shot of his fine tequila, adding to her lassitude. "You weren't really trying and you know it," she said, watching him work his belt through the loops and pull his shirt back on.

"That's true," he said, patting her bottom. "I wouldn't have time to care for you properly after a serious afternoon. I have to get back to the barns." He squatted beside the bed, bringing his face into her line of sight, his chin propped on his forearms. "Are you all right? Can I get you a glass of water, or have them bring you something from the kitchen?"

"I'm lovely. I'll be on my feet in five minutes, no worse for your lame effort." She smiled at him.

"Lame, eh?" He stretched across the mattress and covered her lips with a savage kiss until she pushed him back with a laugh. "Get some rest." He cupped his hand between her legs. "And for now, only I get to touch here, yes? Not you, not anyone else." He curled his finger with suggestive purpose and her nerves glimmered like the trailing sparks of a firework.

"Yes, Javier."

He pushed off the bed and pulled open the dark curtains a few inches. Light flooded in through the sheers, but there was no sign of Ryan. Javier ran his palm over her bottom. "You have tied yourself in knots, Natalie, so let me tell you something," he said, pressing a kiss to the low curve of her spine. He pulled the sheet to her mid back and added a kiss on her shoulder. "You think your submissive nature makes you weak, but you're wrong. You're strong, *cariño*. So strong. I'll see you later, yes? We still have much to discuss."

Natalie listened to Javier's boot steps recede down the hallway outside her door, then turned her head to watch as he clattered down the front stairs outside. He settled his flat-crowned hat onto his head and flicked his wrist in an imperious gesture meant to send the hands in the corral scattering to the corners of the horse-operation.

Natalie sighed. Back to work for them all.

She allowed herself the full five minutes before she got reluctantly out of bed, slipped on a pair of loose pants and a T-shirt, and picked up the weekend agenda Chloe had provided to each of them. There was a lake cruise leaving at four. Natalie glanced at the clock. Nope, she wasn't going to make that, not with the need to catch up at the office. She shot Chloe a text apologizing for her absence and then logged into her office extranet while she dialed her phone. Her assistant, Caroline, answered on the first ring.

"Oh, thank God, Natalie."

"I've got a stable internet connection now," Natalie said without preamble. "Set up a video conference and let's get this sucker handled. Get someone from marketing, PR, and legal. And leave Stanley out of it. He's got everyone freaked out enough as it is." Her boss was great at corporate communication, but far too much the hair-on-fire-type when it came to a marketing mistake that could cost the company millions. Probably something to do with his compensation package.

"Got ya. Twenty minutes? I'll email you the link."

"Ten. Ten minutes, Care. Oh, and get that guy from tech." Natalie wracked her brain but couldn't come up with the name. "The one who's really good at dumbing down his end of things for us. We can come up with all the creative solutions we want, but if tech can't pull it off, we're wasting our time. Vaneesh! That's the one."

"Vaneesh. All right…" Caroline's voice was replaced by the mad background clicking of a keyboard. "Okay, we have an online video con set. You should see the link any second. Invites are all sent."

"Perfect. You're on the call, too."

"I'll be there, boss."

Natalie hung up and hoped they wouldn't notice her standing through the entire meeting.

Chloe had jammed the weekend full of group activities. After the boat tour, they had a dressy dinner, for which Natalie had plenty of time to prepare, physically and mentally. As Chloe's co-maid of honor, she would be sitting at the same table as Ryan. Hopefully somewhere far enough away she could continue to ignore him.

Or not. When she walked into the private dining room, her eye caught him first. To locate him, she told herself, so she could keep the crowd and the width of the room between them. So what if he had glanced up when she entered, as if he'd been watching for her, or if he was holding her gaze like a tractor beam?

She had managed fine on the drive to the lodge. She could manage tonight, and this entire weekend. It only required a conscious decision to break eye contact and scan the rest of the room.

Javier had taken special interest in this space. Original artwork and shelves of Spanish wine lined the walls, and Chloe and Dave's friends ranged out, admiring both. In the center of the room, three tables had been arranged in a "U," the head table set for five, presumably Chloe and Dave, Ryan, the best man, and both maids-of-honor, Natalie, and Jenna, Chloe's best friend. The wine steward stopped in front of Natalie, offering her a glass of champagne. When everyone had been served, Ryan tapped his glass with the tines of a fork, gathering the wedding party's attention and asking everyone to find a seat. Natalie sat on the far end next to Jenna, putting three people between her and Ryan. Perfect.

While everyone settled, Jenna eyed Natalie, and then Ryan, with an inquisitive gaze, one that seemed intent on figuring them out. Obviously, Chloe had spread the word that the two of them had split, but Natalie had no intention of making it a topic of conversation. She turned toward Ryan as he stood. As always, he presented an appealing view, dressed in a crisp blue cotton shirt, tailored slacks, and carefully tamed hair. Of course, all the polish contrasted wildly with his crooked smile, and the mischievous twinkle in his eye. Traits that made him all the more dangerous.

"I'm sure you're all as happy as I am to be part of what, I predict, is going to be an epic union of two incredible people," Ryan said, tipping his glass toward Chloe and Dave. His gaze touched on each of them fondly, then tracked to Natalie, lingering a shade too long. Chloe and Jenna both turned to look at her, but Natalie only offered a bland smile, and kept a neutral eye on Ryan. "May we all be so lucky," he said, raising his glass. The rest of them did likewise with various shouts of good fortune—*cheers* and *skal* and *salud*.

The waitstaff paraded in next, bringing a meal of bison tenderloin, pecan-crusted rainbow trout fished from the local rivers, creamy golden potatoes, and fresh asparagus. How Javier managed to attract five-star-worthy chefs to the isolation of northern Idaho had always been one of the great mysteries of his success.

Spanish guitar floated from speakers overhead, barely

audible above the clink of silverware and lively conversation. Natalie absorbed it all with only half an ear. She didn't mean to be aloof. She loved her sister dearly, but they couldn't be more different, which made socializing with numerous Chloe-alikes a bit of a strain. At least Jenna was easier than the others. She treated Natalie with a sort of respectful fear, and only engaged when Natalie initiated the conversation.

Luckily, the rest of the bridal party talked up a storm, so Natalie didn't feel any responsibility for conversation. All she had to do was occasionally nod or murmur *mm-hmm* to maintain her end.

When the dishes were finally cleared after fresh berry sorbet and chocolate torte, everyone stood and started moving around the room in search of fresh conversational targets. Natalie stayed seated, reveling in a moment of peace.

It was short-lived, though. Ryan pulled an empty chair around and straddled it, facing her. "Are we going to have a standoff every time we see each other?" he asked.

Natalie's brows rose. "Excuse me?"

"Come on, Nat, don't do this."

Me? she almost squawked. She bit her tongue before she made a scene. "I'm not sure I understand why you think we need to be friends, Ryan," she said. "We dated, it didn't work out. Move on."

His cheeks flushed with annoyance. "Dated. That's a nice reconstruction."

Anger bloomed in Natalie's stomach, a hot ball that expanded out until her fingers twitched with the urge to shove him away. "Would you prefer me to say you brought around another woman to fuck?"

"Don't be absurd." He took her wineglass out of her hand before she knew he was reaching for it, and took hold of her wrist. Natalie watched, speechless, as he brought her hand to his mouth and grazed his teeth across her knuckles, his steady gaze daring her to look away. "That isn't what happened and you know it," he whispered. "Talk to me, Nat. What are you afraid of?"

She knew her silence was unfair to him, but she couldn't grapple with what to say, or how to say it.

And then Chloe popped up behind him and grabbed a handful of his shirtsleeve. "Come on, Ryan!" she said, giving a yank. "Tequila shooters. Dave's waiting for you."

Natalie offered her sister a quick, grateful smile. Chloe's bouncy good nature sometimes overshadowed her intelligence, perilous for those who underestimated her. She and Dave had introduced Ryan and Natalie, and though Chloe didn't know exactly what had gone down, she knew enough to perceive Natalie's discomfort.

Ryan let go of Natalie's wrist and stood, but when Chloe wandered over to the makeshift bar set up at one of the other tables, Ryan didn't follow her. Instead, he bent over the back of Natalie's chair, his hand braced on the table, his stubbled jaw against her smooth one. "Tell me about the cowboy, Nat," he murmured.

The entire floor seemed to tip to one side and Natalie blinked it back to level. Her blurry gaze followed the tendons on the back of Ryan's hand to the monogram sewn onto the cuff of his shirt. "What cowboy?" she said, her words as hazy as her vision. "This place is crawling with them."

"The only one who looked at you like he owned you. The one who looked at me like he'd happily see me caught in a stampede. The one who had you blindfolded and begging," he murmured. "What, exactly, was he to you?"

He'd seen through the window after all. Natalie raised her wineglass, amazed she didn't slosh the contents over the tablecloth. She took a long, slow sip before she said, "I don't know what you're talking about."

Ryan prowled into her line of sight and leaned against the

table, his arms crossed. "You know exactly what I'm talking about."

"Really, Ryan. Your interest in my life is unhealthy. That girl—what was her name? Preston, Sawyer, something—she'd be happy to have more of your attention, I'm sure. You're a good fuck."

He rocked back as if he'd been slapped, his brows lowering dangerously. "Since when do you sink to crudity, Natalie?"

Never. She never sank so low. Nor did she understand why she was lashing out, except that she felt like a cornered animal. "Go away, Ryan."

"I will. After you tell me why you're throwing away the last eight months without a backward glance."

Natalie stared while her brain yelled *tell him!* but she couldn't make her lips move. He'd pushed her boundaries without consulting her first, brought a submissive around like a cat bringing his owner a mouse. She clung to her grievance tenaciously, even though it hadn't been his ill-thought action that caused her to bolt. Just the opposite. The sight of the bound woman had made the submissive side of her yearn, offered an easy return to a lifestyle she'd chosen to shut away. All she would have had to do was put out her hands and cross her wrists. Oh, how she had ached to.

She'd spent too long convincing herself she'd made the right choice when she gave that part of her life up. Too long to give in to a moment of weakness. Then or now.

Dammit. She fished under her chair for her clutch and left the room without saying another word.

As she hurried through the main dining room, Javier's words came swirling back to her. *He wants you. Like this.* Natalie shook the voice out of her head. Nope. Ryan was just a typical alpha male. Sure, he exhibited an above-average air of authority and he liked his soft kinks, but he was nothing like Javier. Nothing.

He was not...*that.* Was he?

I would mentor him, Javier had said.

No, no, no. Natalie rushed down the stairs to the lobby. She didn't want this complication, but as she crossed the flagstone floor and heard footsteps behind her, it became obvious she wouldn't outrun it. She glanced back and Ryan caught up with her, herding her into a small alcove fitted out as a coat room.

Natalie spun to face him. "Why are you hounding me, dammit?"

He grasped her upper arms. "You can't just shut down and check out this time, Nat. You have to talk to me."

His hands caressed her bare arms, every stroke making Natalie's back more rigid. "I don't have to," she said.

"You're right, I'm sorry," he said with a sigh, the soft sound stabbing at her. He deserved credit for trying to find patience. "I'm asking you to. Jesus, the ride from Spokane was the most brutal two hours of my life. You and me in the back of a limo. My mind went everywhere, Natalie. I imagined making you sit across from me and spread your legs, telling you to run your finger over the front of your silky panties. I wanted to see the dark line where you touched, and watch your face when you came."

"Oh, don't," she whispered. He had always been gifted at painting these erotic portraits, creating vivid scenes they would often play out, leaving them both laughing and sweaty and riding the high of fantasy-fueled orgasms.

"I miss us, Nat."

She had so little defense against him. Even now, he lit a slow-burning fuse inside her.

"But the next two hours...after I saw you react to that cowboy, after I saw what he was to you? And you to him? Those were so much worse." He skimmed his hands down her arms and wove their fingers together, then raised their clasped hands behind her back until her elbows winged out. Besides restraining her, the maneuver had the added benefit of making her breasts rub against his chest. He looked down, a flash of craving in his off-kilter smile. "I've wanted to make you mine like that from the minute I met you, Nat. I wanted to be the one to make you sit between my thighs, to blindfold you. I wanted to be the one to tie your hands and touch you until you screamed," he said, his lips against her ear. "I handled you with kid gloves because I thought you didn't know what seemed so obvious to me, but it turns out, you've known all along."

She flinched at his wounded tone. "I'm not—whatever you think."

"You were his sub."

Natalie blew a frustrated breath and raised her eyes to meet his. "Was. Not anymore." Saying it out loud didn't make her feel any more certain she could keep the claim.

He inched their hands higher, and she hitched a breath. "I don't think so, Nat. I know the sound of that breath, that look in your eye. I know what I'd find if I reached between your legs."

Natalie turned her head, confused and embarrassed. "Speaking of crude."

"I know," he said. "But I'm not wrong, am I?"

This could not be happening. What higher being had she offended to deserve her life being turned upside down and inside out like this? And in the course of only a few hours.

"Look at me, Natalie," Ryan said, his tone clipped.

Her gaze snapped to his. She couldn't *not* look, not when he spoke to her like that. And all she could think was, how hadn't she seen it before? "We didn't work out, Ryan. Please let it go."

"But we did, babe." He let her arms down. "That's why I don't understand. I did something incredibly stupid. Juvenile, in fact. Just…I have no excuse except I knew there could be so much more for us."

Natalie huffed a laugh, one devoid of humor. "You should have asked first."

"I knew what you'd say. I thought actually seeing it might sway you." He touched his forehead to hers. "Damn, I'm so sorry. I never meant to freak you out. I never wanted to lose you, Nat."

He'd explained all this the day she'd booted him out. She'd heard the words, but now they were cast in a different light. Now that she knew more about him, and about herself. She took in the rosy flush high on his cheeks, the square set of his jaw. Apprehension and anticipation, both.

Whatever Ryan saw in her face, one side of his mouth rose slowly into the rogue's smile that used to set the fluttery things inside her free. The one that invited her to play. He wrapped both her wrists with one strong hand while his other hand cupped her bottom and pulled her close. "What I really wanted in the limo," he said, his voice rough as he nipped along the curve of her ear, "was to bend you over my knee, bare your ass, and for you to turn to me and say, *please*."

Heat surged through her, and Natalie had to close her eyes, waiting for the flood to recede. She wanted to weep with the urge to let him, take his hand and lead him to her room, let him tie her up, bare her, mark her, play out a scene. Even with the ghost of Javier's handprint still on her ass. Damn that Spaniard for reawakening all her darkest impulses.

When the urgency passed, she raised her face and pressed her lips to his. "Please," she whispered. "Don't."

He pulled back, his expression stark, and after a long, silent pause, he let go of her. She couldn't look at him as she slipped past him and fled.

Her heels beat on the floor as she made for her room, desperate to unsee Ryan's wounded gaze. Once there, Natalie curled under a blanket on her chaise and stared into the night. Regardless of what Javier thought, she had managed fine outside of the submissive lifestyle. She wasn't completely fulfilled, but so what? Who the hell was?

Her months with Ryan had been lovely, enhanced by their spicy vanilla sex life. Javier had loved and molded her with his steady dominance, but Ryan made her laugh, and laughed easily himself, allowed her to experience...normal... ish. When their games occasionally made her ache for some of the sharper edges of her life with Javier, for Ryan to take her firmly in hand...well, she reminded herself she'd walked away from being a submissive for a reason.

Not that her reason made much sense at the moment.

Not when her Benedict Arnold of a brain conjured an image of Javier. Rugged and robust, with his air of old patrician entitlement, his rough hands, and sun-drenched skin. Wrapping her wrists in leather, looking down on her as she worshiped him with her mouth. A dominant through and through.

Ryan wavered beside him. Sleek and modern in his tailored suit, the top button of his shirt undone, his hand on her head as she knelt, bound at his feet, his shiny, expensive belt in his fist.

A shiver traced down her spine.

Restless, she went into the bathroom and confronted herself in the mirror. Her secure little box had been flung open, all her secrets, her dark needs and kinky desires, exposed for anyone to see. Yet hadn't she proven today that being a submissive didn't detract one bit from her strong, professional side? Javier and Ryan both seemed to believe she could, should, embrace both.

She had known coming back to Javier's ranch might mean confronting her fears head on. She simply hadn't considered Ryan would be the one to skewer the truth home.

Despite her restless night, Natalie lurched out of bed at gawdawful-o'clock to answer a knock on the door. One of the ranch's young employees rolled in a room service cart with a pot of coffee, fresh berries and croissants, and a wrapped package.

Javier, damn him. He knew her well, but did it have to be so early? She poured a cup and sat down to prod the envelope from under the box's ribbon. Inside, she found a hand-scrawled note.

Come to the barn at 10 wearing this and the things I left in your room yesterday. Check the bedside drawer. I trust by the extraordinary weight of your suitcase you brought your boots. ~J

Natalie unwrapped the box and drew out a short-sleeved, flower-printed prairie dress. She rubbed the fine fabric between her thumb and fingers, lost in thought again. She'd spent most of the night tossing and turning, contemplating both Javier's statement of her strengths and Ryan's question of her fears. Now, by the light of day, she had to admit she had been silly. The only question left was what she intended to do about it. She held the dress out at arm's length. Maybe, just maybe, she could let her submissive side out of the cage, just for a weekend.

She slid open the bedside table drawer and found the sexiest panties she'd ever laid eyes on. The front was demure enough. Dark gray netting that would mostly cover her girl bits, pretty black lace along the leg, and a thin fuchsia band along the top edge. But the back was something else entirely. The lace continued around the leg, but above that there was… not much. Six pink strings formed a sort of web, connected at the waist with a black bow. And crotchless, of course. The fuchsia satin bra was entirely tame by comparison.

She looked down at the note and drew a deep breath. She would go to Javier and make sure he understood that yesterday, and whatever was to come today, was temporary— for this weekend only. She'd deal with Ryan later.

After a long bath and another hour of primping, Natalie left her room and meandered to the corrals, earlier than Javier had directed.

She found him working a gorgeous black stallion whose scraggly bangs covered his eyes and reached half the length of his nose. The horse, high-stepping and dancing on his lead, had trouble written all over him. Javier whistled sharply, an affront to the animal that resulted in an elegant but dangerous pivot on his rear legs. The move had Javier ducking and cursing the headstrong stallion's entire maternal lineage.

Natalie grinned and propped her elbows on the top rail to watch the war of wills. "I could learn something from him," she said when Javier shouldered the horse's flank on another prancing twirl.

"Don't encourage him," Javier growled. "He's showing off."

"Is he?" Natalie turned and spied the real trouble at the opposite end of the corral complex. "Oh, she's a beauty."

"He thinks so," Javier said, grunting. He gave another sharp whistle and the randy horse shook his mane but finally settled.

"Maybe you shouldn't have corralled her upwind," Natalie said, her brows raised.

Javier graced her with his most severe expression, one she'd seen even his seasoned employees shrink from. "Your opinion is duly noted," he said, annoyance making his accent so pronounced his English grew almost impossible to understand.

Trying not to grin, Natalie shrugged and pulled an imaginary zipper across her lips. When the stallion started up again, Javier called over his shoulder. "Make yourself useful, would you? Walk her to the back barn. And be sure you secure the door. *Madre de dios, hijo!*" he snapped, yanking down on the stallion's lead as the horse reared again.

Natalie strolled up to the docile mare, who appeared entirely uninterested in the stallion's antics. As Javier had taught her, Natalie let the horse smell her hand and spoke to her in a low monotone before hooking the rope he had left dangling from the fence rail onto her halter. The two of them ambled to the smaller back barn Javier kept for breeding and foaling. Natalie led the mare to the largest stall, gave her a slightly withered carrot from a coffee can outside the gate, and locked her inside. By the time she returned to the corral, both Javier and the stallion were gone, but the barn door stood partially open.

She wandered into the airy, high-ceilinged building. Javier took great pride in his barn. The elite horse breeders of Spain boasted centuries of tradition, and pride dictated maintaining their horses in luxurious conditions, even in Idaho. *We must show them how deeply we care for them if we expect them to carry us through peril*, Javier had once told her. *No different than the way one treats a lover.*

Two horses nearest the door poked their noses over their stall doors and sniffed the air. She didn't recognize either of them. Javier had replenished his stock since she'd been here last.

"They're flirting, those two." Javier's voice floated from the far end of the barn, along with the squeak and clink of a saddle and the scrape of his boot heels across the floor. "Don't give them any attention for it."

"These rascals, too?" Ignoring Javier's grousing, she reached out to rub one silky nose. The gorgeous Paint blew a wet sniff onto her hand then breathed it back, taking her measure.

"They're horny. What do you expect?" Javier approached from down the long aisle. He'd thrown on his shirt, but hadn't bothered to button it and sweat dripped enticingly down his chest as he toted his saddle in front of him, his hands hidden by blankets and the dangling fender. He whistled through his teeth. Natalie snatched her hand back as the colt flung up his head and shook his mane in irritation before he shuffled back from the gate.

"At least this one minds better," she said.

"He's much stupider than the wild man out there. Sit down, *cariño*," Javier said, raising his chin toward a spot behind her.

Natalie looked around. There was only one so-called seat, a hay bale pushed against the wall outside the office door. It would make an uncomfortable place for his employees to wait should *Señor* Vazquez wish to see them. Which was probably the point. Natalie perched on the edge of the bale.

"Real cowboy work this morning?" She glanced from his hat to his chaps to his dusty boots.

He almost smiled. "The dress is nice. Sit back, *cariño*. Spread your legs, pull your skirt over your knees."

She looked up, judging his intent. "Javier—"

He twitched his head, questioning her small defiance.

Sighing, she gathered the fabric and drew it over her knees. "Where are all the hands? It's awfully quiet in here for this time of the morning."

"They're on the trails getting the overlook cleaned up. Your sister asked for cocktail hour with a view." His head tilted, as if he might see further under her dress. "*Dios mío.* Is there anything more alluring than the shadow between a woman's thighs?"

Natalie had to distract him until they could discuss her limits. "Is that what Chloe has planned? Won't it be dark when we come down?"

"We'll have lamps," Javier said, his voice gravely. "Higher, *cariño*."

"You're drunk on horse hormones," she said. Still, she tugged the hem higher.

"If I were, I'd have been over your back with my cock in you by now."

"Javier," she said, trying to ignore the rush of sensation low in her belly.

His laugh rumbled in the hush of the barn even after he disappeared into the tack room.

Weary from her sleep-deprived night, Natalie stretched out across the length of the bale and watched the lazy golden motes that hung suspended in the wide rays of sunlight slanting inside. She dozed in the warm, horsey air, and the next thing she knew, Javier returned, tugging on a fresh shirt and wearing clean jeans. He ruffled his fingers through his wet hair and sprayed her with fine droplets.

"Wake up, *cariño*."

"I'm awake," she grumbled.

He grasped her knees and ran his hands up her thighs, taking her dress with them. "There is what I was trying to see," he said, eyeing the scrap-of-nothing underwear. "Very risqué." He drew his thumb across the net fabric, then leaned down to place a kiss where his thumb had pressed. "Why are you napping? Didn't you sleep well last night?"

Natalie glared at him. "As a matter of fact, I didn't."

He swung her legs off the bale and sat in the vacant space. "Come here, grumpy girl," he said quietly, settling her against his chest. His fingers drew over her head in slow, relaxing spirals.

She'd missed these small things, his gruff, affectionate touch, hearing his accent strengthen as passion overtook him. She tucked her nose against his chest and inhaled, in search of his irresistible musk, hidden under bright laundry soap.

"I understand there was a small confrontation with your Ryan last night."

"Are you having me watched, Javier?"

"Of course, *cariño*. You think I would not keep an eye on you while you're here?" His fingers twirled and twirled, and a taut silence spun out between them. "Do you still love him?"

Natalie fiddled with his buttons, turning one to slide through a hole and then pulling it back, over and over. "You know me, Javier. I don't seem able to fall *out* of love. But if you're asking if I want him back... Yesterday, I would have said no."

"And today?"

"Today, it's complicated."

"Why, Natalie? He is young, and he is a city slicker." The phrase, spoken in his heavy accent, made her chuckle. "He can be for you what I cannot."

"What?" Natalie said, pushing upright. She straddled his thighs and gave him a close look. "Of course he can't. He could never be you. Don't be crazy." She tapped him on the temple.

He pulled her finger away, then bit down on it. "You know what I mean. He's there, I'm here."

She opened her mouth to argue, but he gave his head a small shake. "I let you go because you wanted it, Natalie, even though I didn't. Now I find you lost and unhappy. I'm concerned, *cariño*. I think, but for a forgivable mistake, your Ryan made you happy."

"Forgivable," Natalie said with a snort. She combed her fingers through Javier's hair, smoothing it down the way he liked it. "I'm not unhappy. I am unnerved by being here, I'll grant you. And Ryan seems determined not to go away without a fuss."

Javier drew a finger along the heart-shaped neckline of her dress. "I told you he wants you."

"Why does it matter to you?"

"Because, *cariño*, you need someone who appreciates both sides of you. I watched him. He likes your sexy business clothes, and the way you are with the phone in your hand, intense and focused on your work."

She gaped at him. "Javier, you've done nothing but mark your territory since I stepped foot onto this ranch. Now you're trying to convince me to take Ryan back? Which is it?"

His gaze touched every part of her face. "Can't it be both?"

He might as well have injected a hypodermic of hormones straight into her vein, so instantly did her body react. His hands moved to her breasts, cradled them, fondled nipples that stood out as if she'd been dipped in an icy mountain lake. Between her legs, she was flushed and ready as any mare in heat.

"Not an idea you'd dismiss, then?" he whispered, kissing her lips, her chin, and the soft places under her jaw.

Two days ago she would have, before the barriers she'd erected had all been breached. Now her heart insisted on honesty, even if her mouth wouldn't cooperate.

Javier's hands slipped under her skirt, and he wound his fingers in the strings crossing her bottom. He pulled her snug against him. "I knew I'd like these. I can wind my fingers in them like reins."

Her breasts brushed his chest as she inhaled a stuttering breath, and when she still hadn't answered, he took hold of her hair and pulled slowly down, raising her chin to make her look at him. What he saw made his skin flush a ruddy bronze and his pupils dilate, turning his eyes from green to glittering black.

"Up, *pequeña*." His tone dared her to defy him.

Defiance was the last thing on her mind. She scrambled off his lap, and he backed her against the wall outside the

Paint's stall. The raw pine pricked her skin and the scent of straw enveloped her as Javier's boots crushed stalks on the floor.

With urgent hands, and without a word, he bound her wrists using one of the reins dangling from the tack hook and then spun her around and raised her tied wrists over the hook. "Feet back, *pequeña*," he ordered, his voice raspy, his actions brisk. Natalie watched over her shoulder as he drew off his shirt, her body equally restless, her soul aching for him to take her, break her. He pulled her hips back farther, flattening her spine. Gathering her skirt across her waist, he bared her from ass to knees.

"*Madre de dios*," he whispered, his palm drifting over her bottom and down to the top of her thigh. His thumb dragged enticingly over her center.

Natalie's eyes closed as she imagined how she must look to him, the curves of her bottom crisscrossed by the thin strings of the panties, and below, framed by black lace, her body flaunting itself, parting, taunting him with what lay deeper.

Javier sucked a breath through his teeth as his fingertips slid through her lush flesh, teasing her, making promises as he pressed deep between her legs. His other hand ran the length of her arm and closed over the leather binding her wrist, his muscled forearm stretching alongside her more delicate one. He scraped her cheek with his chin. "Did you mind me, *pequeña*?" His voice rumbled through her, a fine vibration from the top of her scalp to the base of her spine. "Even when you shaved your *conejo*, you didn't give in to temptation?"

"No, Javier." Her words were no more a sound than the shuffling of horses in their stalls.

He paused, the stillness of his fingers tormenting her. "Why not, *mi pequeña*?"

"Because you told me not to." She inhaled sharply as his

fingers glided past her clit.

"Good girl. Did you give your Ryan the same respect, I wonder?" Javier mused as he rose from her back.

Natalie stilled. She didn't want to discuss Ryan anymore, but Javier was apparently determined to have his say. "He didn't ask for that sort of respect."

Javier's belt buckle clinked behind her, ratcheting her nerves until the prickling over her exposed flesh felt like bubbles in a champagne glass, all chasing in one direction.

Fingers strong enough to control a stallion clamped on to her hips. "I didn't ask for it, either," he said. "I took it." He thrust inside her, hit bottom in one stroke, the buttons of his jeans spurring into the backs of her thighs.

Pain, bright and transitory, was chased away almost immediately by intense pleasure as he drove deep inside her. He knew her physical limits—they'd learned them together— even if it seemed he was intent on skating the edge this morning. He followed with another deep thrust that rocked her forward, made her gasp. "I should never have let you go," he said, his voice tight. "I should have spirited you off to Spain and kept you for myself."

Natalie turned her cheek to the wall and let Javier propel her toward the opaque margins where her awareness dissolved, where her body became white space marked only with bright splashes, the colors of pleasure and pain. It had been so long since she'd been there.

She wanted it like a drug.

But just as she began to climb, Javier ceased all movement, held utterly still deep within her, dragging her back from the soft emptiness. "No you don't, Natalie."

"Fuck," she groaned, earning herself a stinging smack on her ass.

"Don't be a *puta*," he said. "You know I expect better."

The imprint of his hand throbbed, warm and tingling,

the sensation scattering to all her sensitive places. This was his way, the sublime winding and unwinding of pleasure, controlling both her ascent into subspace and her sexual response, until he gave her permission to have either, or both. She was never to fly there on her own, but she was woefully out of practice.

And too close to tolerate his restriction gracefully.

She stared at a knot in the pine, forced herself to wait him out, through the trembling of her knees and her mind yelling *fuck me!*

Finally he drew back, slow and controlled. "I know, *cariño.* You've been a long time without any direction." His voice was deceptively calm, soothing even. With a swift surge, he drove her onto her toes, only this time he didn't relent. The slap of their skin and their jagged, breathy moans were not quiet. On the other side of the wall, the horse grew restive, whinnying and thumping the stall under Natalie's cheek, wound up by the flood of pheromones and the ferrous smell of sex and the need in her cries. Javier wound a fistful of her hair, pulled back on her head, and arched her back, changing the angle and driving somehow deeper. His pace slowed, but the power in each thrust rose. "It has been more than a year since I've been with a woman, Natalie. You owe me for every day of it."

Her lungs burned and seized, and her heart stopped beating for what felt like too long, and then raced too fast, until she thought it would burst. Vertigo swamped her and she wanted to beg, but dared not. She clenched her fists, her nails digging into her palms.

"Who will be first, *pequeña,* me or you?" Javier asked, his voice ragged. He reached around her hip and thrust his fingers under the flimsy netting of the underwear he'd gifted her, across her clit, taking full possession of her, buffeting her from behind, gliding hot and smooth both in front and inside, wringing her tighter, pushing animal sounds up her throat.

Her legs threatened to collapse under his weight as he bent forward to reach again for her wrist, his sweat-glazed skin sliding feverish and slick on hers. "I can't," she breathed. "I can't."

"You can," he said, and with a feral growl, he poured himself into her, his cock pulsing, contracting, his fingers stroking, urgent and demanding. "*Cariño*," he moaned.

Her ears rang and then muted as he broke her in a tumbling, mindless tide. She was vaguely aware of her cries, and of the fading echoes of his name when she could hear again.

Javier's breathing rasped against her ear, competing with her own, and he held her upright with his hand cupped between her legs, absorbing the pulsing remnants of her climax. She rested her head on his bicep and bathed in the musky heat emanating off him, too drained to speak. She would have bruises to show for that barrage, and the thought pleased her.

A scrape and a footstep sounded from behind them. Javier froze a second and then took his weight off her back. "*Hola*, what can I do for you?" he said, twitching Natalie's skirt around them to give her a modicum of cover.

"What can you do for me?" said a harsh but familiar voice.

Natalie went rigid and glanced under her arm. Ryan. Standing there in his familiar black urban work boots and dark jeans with neatly turned cuffs, the sleeves of his oxford shirt rolled haphazardly. He stared at her bound wrists, then caught her spying and frowned at her with rank discontent. And naked craving.

Natalie's inner muscles clenched.

"I felt that," Javier whispered, nipping her ear. She rocked against him in silent rebuke, and he canted his hips back, letting himself slip from inside her. Her dress ruffled all the way down and Javier righted his jeans.

"You summoned me," Ryan said through gritted teeth. "At this specific time."

"Sorry, *cabrón*. Natalie arrived early and distracted me. Now is not a good time anymore." He unwound Natalie's wrists with careful fingers.

"The fuck it isn't," Ryan replied, scowling down at her hands as she shook the blood back into them. He pinned her with a bristling gaze. "I think now is the perfect time."

"And I think you have some things to learn," Javier said, redirecting Ryan's scrutiny. "Manners, for one. Self-control, for another."

Ryan's cheeks flushed deep red. Impatiently, he raked back the dark strands of hair that had fallen alongside his face, but he held his tongue.

Javier nodded in approval. "As you know from my message, I have a proposal for you." He glanced at Natalie.

Her mouth flattened. They hadn't spoken about anything so specific as a *proposal*.

"But now I don't have time to discuss it, *hijo*. I have work to do."

"So you called me down here to make sure I know you've got your claim staked. I figured it out yesterday, *cabrón*."

Javier's expression flattened. He swept his shirt off the floor and snapped bits of straw off it, then tipped his head toward Natalie. "If you would be so kind as to walk her back up to the lodge?" With every expectation of compliance, he strode into his office and shut the door with a quiet *click*.

Natalie muttered about dominant pricks as Ryan stepped close, crowding her.

"What is this all about?"

"You think I know?" Natalie snapped.

"I think you know more than I do."

She probably did, but not enough to provide an answer that would satisfy him. She turned away and barged into Javier's office to make use of the bathroom. Minutes later, she emerged without a word to either man, but when she tried to brush past Ryan, he grabbed hold of her hand and led her away. They wove between the corrals and headed up the hill to the lodge in silence, but just as she was about to dash up the front stairs he said, "Sit down, Nat. You're going to talk to me. Five minutes." He waved to the Adirondack chairs arrayed along the wide porch, and Natalie flushed. This was the spot he'd watched her from yesterday.

There was no avoiding him. Not now, and she wasn't sure she wanted to. Javier's question—*why can't it be both?*—had taken root with alarming ease, and the covetous look on Ryan's face in the barn had made something needy writhe inside her.

She settled onto one of the chairs where the sun could beat down on her legs, but Ryan pulled up a curved footrest and sat with his shadow cast over her. He clasped his hands between his knees, as if to keep himself from touching her, perhaps declaring a small truce.

He leaned forward and his hair fell once again to brush his cheek. Natalie had to stifle the urge to smooth it back for him.

"I want to fucking throttle you, Nat," he stated.

Okay, not a truce, then. She watched him in steady silence.

"No, I want to tie you up and make you—" A growl of frustration rattled in his throat. "I knew, dammit, but you made me second-guess myself. Why?"

She raised her knees under her skirt and traced a finger randomly through the cornflowers printed on the fabric. "Because I walked away from being someone's sub, Ryan. It was my past, and that's where I wanted it to live."

He braceleted her wrist with a loose grasp. When she looked up, he caught her gaze and held it. "Do you remember that party for Aquator last winter? At that penthouse on the eastside?"

She didn't even have to think. The night remained a vivid picture. Isaac, Ryan's company's major shareholder, had arrived with his date looking like they'd just stepped out of a magazine shoot. He wore a black suit and crisp starched shirt, his cuff links flashing gold and lapis, everything about him perfectly groomed. But it had been the woman who arrested Natalie's attention. Tall, willowy, her hair jet black and adamantly straight, the ends and fringe both cut in hard, straight lines. The corner of a tattoo had peeked from the neckline of her black velvet dress, and her three-quarters sleeves had revealed a velvet bracelet.

And attached to the bracelet, a silver chain.

Isaac and the woman never stood more than a few inches apart, their arms always touching. Not because they were overly affectionate, but because he held the chain tight in his fist.

"You were watching her all night," Ryan said, his thumb tracking back and forth over the underside of Natalie's wrist. "I thought the grief on your face was because you felt bad for her. But now I know. It wasn't for her. It was for you."

She stared hard at him, straining her eyes wide against the sting of tears.

Ryan brought her hand to his mouth, held her immobile with nothing but his steady regard. "Do you long for something around your wrist, Natalie, with a silver chain a man can hold you by?"

All manner of chemicals dumped into her bloodstream, leaving her feverish and prickly, needing to flee and desperate to stay.

He tugged her arm, pulling her forward as he leaned

closer, too. He nipped at her bottom lip, then cupped his hand behind her head and kissed her with a gentleness that felt dangerous. "Ask me to your room, Nat."

She pulled her head back, feeling sick inside. "I just fucked another man, Ryan."

He wound his fingers in her hair. "I know, babe. I'd like to make you forget."

She swayed in his grasp. *Boundaries*, she reminded herself. She had to establish her boundaries. She hadn't gotten the chance with Javier, and she couldn't make the same mistake again. "I don't know what I want, Ryan. Javier is one thing. We were together too long to expect him to change how he treats me, but you and I... I don't know if I—"

When she didn't go on, he sat back, his expression a puzzle of hurt and hope. "I won't ask you, Natalie. Submission is a gift, something offered, a gift I have to earn. But I want you to know, while I'm not as experienced as your guy, I'm not exactly green, either. I can be everything he is to you if you want it. Did you know he had a note delivered to my room, asking me to meet the two of you to discuss what he's calling a mentorship? Him mentoring me, I presume." His brows told her what he thought of Javier's tactics.

"Not the specifics, no. He told me the idea in more general terms."

Ryan pressed a kiss into her palm and closed her fingers over it. "Nothing would make me happier than to try again, Nat, but I have to be truthful. I know too much now. I can't go back to vanilla."

"I understand." Her insides churned. She owed him full disclosure, too. "Javier has more in mind for the three of us than mentoring."

Ryan's gaze sharpened. "Does he?"

Natalie nodded. "I'll admit, my interest is piqued. I'm just not sure how I feel about it as a long-term arrangement."

"Intriguing. I suppose I'll listen to him." He sat in silent contemplation a moment, and Natalie didn't intrude. Finally he said, "I won't try to influence your decision, Nat, but I gotta say, I'm having trouble understanding your fear of your submissive side." He cupped her face and ran a gentle thumb across her cheek. "It's fucking beautiful on you."

Without another word, he stood, spearing his hands into his pockets, and ambled away.

Natalie watched him go, her heart simultaneously swelling and breaking into tiny bits. How could she love two men? Want to submit to both? But she did, that much was undeniable.

Natalie returned to her room and scanned the agenda for the afternoon's entertainment—a trail ride she wouldn't be taking. Not after her morning's activities. She contemplated the spa trip to Sandpoint, but the call of an afternoon in blissful isolation made her happier. What she didn't want to do was think about Javier, Ryan, and her. Just for a while. She could take to the woods, or hole up in her room. Or both. Nothing wrong with both. Room first, woods later. She made a quick call to the front desk, asking them to cancel her spa appointment, then stretched out on her bed, and fell immediately back to sleep.

Only the arrival of housekeeping kept her from spending the entire day under the heap of warm blankets. It was three o'clock when they woke her. She took her laptop and left the room to the two women, in search of a pick-me-up. She'd need one if she was going to make it through the night's festivities.

Javier always provided fresh coffee in the lobby for his guests. Filling a paper cup, Natalie took it outside, where a sunny spot and a lounge chair were calling her name. She woke her phone, meaning to clean up her inbox, and maybe poke her nose in her social media accounts, but the birds and the warm breeze overtook her. With her phone in her lap, and the half-drunk coffee on the ground below her, she closed her eyes and absorbed the heat of the day in half consciousness.

Rob woke her this time, stomping up in his boots and hat, a length of rein in his hand. "You missed the ride," he said.

"I've ridden around this ranch plenty of times," Natalie replied, then clamped her lips together. She'd never confided in her siblings about her years-long relationship with Javier. "What's with the rein?"

Rob lifted his hand as if he'd forgotten it was there. "Oh, just…doing some repair."

Natalie raised her brows. "You do know there are people here to do that." When Rob's only response was to shift his feet, she shoved herself out of the chaise. "You're so weird. Get a horse, would you?"

"Working on it."

She strolled away, back to her room to get ready for the evening's activity, martinis at sunset on the rocky promontory overlooking the lake, then back to the ranch for a barbeque. At least it was casual.

After a shower and a change of clothes, Natalie met up with the others out front. Javier stood at the head of a line of horses while the ranch hands went around adjusting saddles and bridles as, one by one, the bridal party was hoisted on horseback.

"You're kidding, right?" Natalie muttered to him. "No one's going to be able to ride down after martinis."

Javier glanced at her. "You don't think I'd risk my horses, do you?"

"Oh, of course. Your horses, not your guests." Natalie smiled and gestured to the flurry of activity. "What's this, then?"

"You ride up, we bring you down in the wagons."

"Great," Natalie said, grimacing. "That oughta be comfy."

"I'll make sure there's a special cushion for you. Is your bottom still tender?" he said, giving her a stealthy pat on the ass.

Natalie turned to face him, but he was scanning conspicuously over her head, examining the progress down the line. "Arrogant man," she said.

He didn't reply, but Natalie didn't miss the twitch of his lips.

Javier boosted Natalie onto one of the last horses, then jerked his chin at the lead rider, staying behind as he sent his guides to lead the party up the hillside. When they arrived at the overlook, everyone was predictably wowed by the view, but Natalie was more interested in the improvements. Javier had installed a metal barrier fence along the edge, suggesting he made more public use of the area than he used to. He'd taken her—in every sense of the word—up here more than once.

After giving the guests the lay of the land, pointing out the outhouses, and warning people to stay on the rocky clearing, most of the ranch workers led the stock down. One stayed behind as combination chaperone and bartender, serving them out of a portable bar stocked with premixed martinis and all the condiments.

As the party roared to life, Natalie strolled among the guests, slowly circling her way toward the tree line, where granite gave way to soil. Her memories, and her desires, intruded, brought to life by the crunch of pine straw underfoot and the smell of resin rising on warm air.

Javier had shown her every inch of the ranch. They'd had sex in meadows and rocky pools of streams, she'd been tied to trees, knelt at Javier's feet in the snow, and been denied orgasms while riding with him on horseback. They had spent the night under the stars up here on the overlook, where he made creative use of pine needles, pine cones, and other natural implements of sensual torture. Here at the ranch, she'd felt feral and untethered and glorious. Powerful in her own way.

She ran her fingers along the trunk of a stunted pine and they came away sticky. "Dammit," she said, rubbing her fingertips with her thumb.

"Problem?" a familiar voice asked.

A feeling of pleasant surrender washed over her as she looked up at Ryan. "A sticky one," she said. "Har-har."

He took possession of her hand and examined her trouble. "Chloe's wondering where you wandered off to."

"She doesn't know I've spent a lot of time here." Natalie looked out toward the sunset reflecting off the water through the trees. "I needed a minute to wrestle with the memories."

"You and he were together a long time. I'm jealous."

"You didn't seem very jealous. Earlier."

"You're right. That was more arousing than I expected it to be. This is the other kind of jealousy." He dug a handkerchief out of his pocket. "The kind where he's had something I wanted."

"Oh." Natalie looked up at him but what more could she say?

"Anyway, here." Spreading her fingers, Ryan poured his martini on them, careful to keep the mess clear of them both. Then he did his best to wipe off the pitch.

"Huh," she said, feeling around where the stickiness had been "That kind of worked."

"Three kinds of booze in one drink makes for a good solvent."

"Apparently. Can't be great on the stomach lining. Thank you. I'm glad you're so old-fashioned you still carry a hanky, even though it's gross."

"From what I can tell, you have a thing for old-fashioned."

Natalie didn't know quite how to respond to that, either.

They both stood there, unsure of each other. Ryan skimmed his fingers through his hair. "I'm glad you're at least willing to talk to me, even if it's awkward. I wasn't sure you would."

"I know. I owe you—"

He shook his head. "Not now. Just…let me enjoy my relief."

When she nodded, he pushed a wayward strand of hair back from her face. Then his lips were against her skin, in that soft spot in front of her ear. A gentle kiss, almost chaste, but not. She shivered. God, she wanted more, so much more, but she just stood there, paralyzed as a frightened animal, holding her breath so as not to give herself away.

"Don't worry," he said softly. "Even though I want you on your knees so badly I ache, my promise this morning still applies. I won't push you."

He stepped back, and after examining her a moment longer, left her standing alone.

"But what if I want you to," Natalie whispered as she watched him hike the short way back to the overlook. At the last minute, he stopped, turned his head, and crooked a finger at her. She didn't hesitate. She followed him back to the party.

As he said he would, Ryan maintained a respectful distance all evening, except for small, incidental-seeming touches—the brush of his fingers on the stem of her martini glass, his palm on her hip as he passed behind her through conversational groups. He managed to be both circumspect and achingly tempting. Finally, as the sun went down in a blaze of beautiful colors, two of the ranch hands returned with a wagon pulled by two draft horses to carry the martini-fueled group downhill through the last of the twilight. When

Ryan squeezed in next to her for the ride, her pleasure almost overwhelmed her discretion.

Call her contrary, greedy, even, but beyond all good sense, she wanted her men back in her life. Both of them.

The wagon required a more winding route down the hill, and they jounced along like pioneers, with half the guys snoring and most of the women complaining. Bitterly.

"Give it a rest, Chloe," Natalie said. "If you were on horseback, you'd be complaining your manicure would be ruined."

"A manicure is totally different," Chloe said. "Massages, Nat. Massages were had. And now I have more kinks in my back than I did when I woke up this morning!"

"Her kinks got nothin' on yours," Ryan muttered into Natalie's ear, earning an elbow to the ribs and a sidelong glare. She caught the flash of his teeth as he grinned.

Chloe glanced from Natalie to Ryan and back again, with a speculative squint. "You didn't say your back hurt, Nat. You should have come with us."

"My back is fine. I had other things to do today." She twitched when Ryan bumped her with his elbow.

"Bleh. You work too much," Chloe said and flopped against a sleeping Dave. "You need to relax more." Her head lolled on his chest with every sway of the wagon, the ride finally lulling almost everyone into a stupor.

"Yeah, Natalie. Let me help you relax," Ryan whispered, his breath warm against her ear. "Know what I'm imagining right now? You in those fuck-me panties. They were the sexiest thing I've ever seen you wear. A luscious cage for your ass."

"You might see them up close. Someday," Natalie said, his description making her smile.

He took her bottom lip between his, tugged and licked, his kiss turning up the heat in the cooling night air. "Did you know a male horse sticks his nose right against the mare's backside when she's in heat?"

"What?" she said with a confused laugh.

"I watched it today when I went back to talk to your cowboy. The stallion stuck his nose right up under her tail."

"Ryan." Natalie laid her fingers over his lips.

He licked them and she drew her hand away. "His head went all tilt-a-whirl, like the smell gave him an instant high. And then he let out this frustrated groan."

"Oh God, please don't imitate it," Natalie whispered.

His low laugh rumbled through her. "I couldn't do it justice. And as you know, I'm more of a snarler." He bared his teeth and skimmed his hand up her ribs, his thumb brushing across her breast, his touch sizzling through her veins.

He wove his fingers through her hair, and his lips grazed her cheek, lingering on the same spot in front of her ear as earlier. The one that made tiny waves ripple under her skin. "I'm going to do it, Nat. I'm going to stick my face between your legs and breathe you in until I'm high. And then I'm going to tie you over a table, and I'm going to take you like that stallion did the mare, until I can't fucking stand up anymore."

Craving oozed through her, made her feel thick and slow everywhere. Her head dropped against his, and she brushed her nose along his jaw. There was no middle ground left between them now that he knew. There was only yes or no.

"Will you want me quiet and docile as a mare?" Natalie asked.

His fingers tensed on her scalp. "Maybe. Maybe sometimes I'll want you begging and writhing. The louder the better."

The throb between her legs was sharp and instant. Natalie clamped her lips to smother her moan, but Dave gave a suspicious flinch and grumbled, "For fuck's sake" under his breath, implying she failed miserably.

Ryan looked at her, his smile sultry. "If we were alone I'd take care of that for you," he said, adding a shrug as if to say, *alas*. He drew his tongue across the seam of her lips, then settled back against the side of the wagon, folded his arms across his chest, and closed his eyes, looking deceptively like an innocent man.

With a shake of her head, Natalie leaned against his shoulder to watch the stars through the bobbing pine branches, and let the rhythmic clop of hooves hypnotize her as they descended the trail. It wasn't until the lodge came into view that the full impact of what Ryan had said about the stallion hit her like a knock to the head.

He'd been in the breeding shed. With Javier. Which meant they had talked, which meant Ryan now probably knew more about what Javier had in mind than she did.

Her heart raced with a terrible mix of anticipation and trepidation. If she wanted to take Javier up on his idea, it would have to be now or never. A fact brought home when the wagon driver handed her a note as he helped her down. Another summons, this time to one of the cabins.

The wedding party rallied for dinner—barbeque and burgers around the fire pit—but Natalie sat quiet, lost in her thoughts. Ryan maintained a solid presence by her side, and Dave and Chloe kept looking at her as if to say, *about time*, but the friendly gathering only made Natalie feel more and more the outsider. Most of the conversation revolved around jobs, condos, and the Seattle bar scene, while Natalie was busy contemplating the pros and cons of returning to submission, engaging in a ménage, and the intense sexual thrill she experienced knowing her intimacies were being observed.

A niggling sense of immorality had her nibbling her thumbnail as the realities descended on her like a weighted blanket. She, of all people, worried about old-fashioned morals. Kind of a joke, but there it was. One voice in her head accused her of shamelessly wanting her cake and eating it, too. Another worried about getting outed somehow. Deep down she knew what she, Javier, and Ryan might engage in wasn't wrong, not if they were all in accord. Her heart wanted it. "I think," she murmured.

If only she could get her head out of the way.

When the tequila started making the rounds, Natalie declined, sticking with the Spanish Tempranillo, but the wine darkened her thoughts even more, let the worries and what-ifs turn from a trickle she could reason herself out of, to a cascade. She stared at Chloe, her ease with Dave, the small touches she didn't have to hide. Natalie wasn't sure she'd ever be able to have that, to commit to one person and know she'd made the perfect choice. To do so, she would have to choose one man over the other. One would always have to represent her public self, the other she could never acknowledge, except in private. She would be living a public lie.

Unless the worst happened, and her private life became public. She'd be a pariah at work, a job she loved and was good at. And her friends... God, what would they think? Natalie didn't even want to contemplate it, or how her parents would react. She felt herself shrinking in her seat.

She knew other people maintained polyamorous relationships, but why would she invite such complications? Three days ago, she would have said she had finally learned how not to have either Javier or Ryan in her life. She had found a level of equilibrium, at the very least. So what was she even thinking about, contemplating not just sex, but a potential relationship with two men? *These* two men. Pure insanity.

The conclusion made her heart stutter, in the way only cold truth could. She pulled Javier's note from her pocket and unfolded it. The scribble only told her where to meet, nothing else. There was no indication he wanted anything more than a repeat of this morning. Except he had met with Ryan. Not an idle encounter.

Natalie glanced across the fire at Ryan talking to one of the other groomsmen, and her throat tightened. She couldn't have everything she wanted. The thought of living with fears and worries, the fact that she was already second-guessing herself, said it all.

She had to tell Javier no. Him and Ryan, both.

When the party got raucous enough she could leave the fire pit unnoticed, Natalie slipped through the shadows behind the lodge, heading uphill to the cabins.

The sound of a breaking branch made her squeak and turn.

Ryan grabbed her by the waist. "C'mere, you. I want you to myself for a minute. I have a feeling it's going to be a lot of watching and not much else for me tonight." He kissed her with all the pent-up tension of the last few hours, or weeks, perhaps, but when he pulled back, Natalie clung to his shoulders. "What? Nat, what's wrong?"

"I can't, Ryan." Natalie heard the quaver in her own voice.

He took hold of both of her hands. "Can't what, babe?"

"I can't do this. I can't have you both, and I can't choose, and—"

"Whoa, stop. Natalie." Ryan ducked his head to look closely at her. "Take a deep breath."

He waited for her to do so, and when she let it out, she

nodded, feeling a touch calmer. At least her head had stopped whirring.

"Nothing is set in stone," he said, his thumbs tracing over the backs of both hands, soothing her. "Nothing. This meeting is just—"

"Meeting? I didn't know it was a meeting."

Ryan shook his head in annoyance. "He didn't tell you what was up? Imperious bastard."

"He sent me a note to come up to the cabin. I assumed..." She gazed off into the middle distance. "I don't know what I assumed. So many things."

"I knew you were looking queasy at the barbeque. I thought it was all the s'mores."

Natalie snorted and looked up at him, at the gentle tease in his eyes, and his lopsided smile. He always used humor to diffuse her tension in just the right way.

"We're only at the *discussing potentials* stage," he assured her. When she nodded again, he added, "I'm sorry he left you to fill in the blanks. Not cool."

Or maybe Javier expected her to know he'd never do anything to hurt her, would never compromise her in any way. She had eight years of knowledge of him to back the assumption. He'd shown only grace, no rancor, when he let her walk away from him, contrary to his own desires. Because she'd wanted it.

She shook her head at her own irrational spiral. "It's not entirely his fault," she said. "You're right, I made assumptions. But, Ryan..." Natalie pressed her lips together, unsure how to say more without hurting him all over again.

"Just wait. Don't say anything." He towed her through a crunchy patch of fallen needles under a towering pine. The moon shone through the trees in bright patches, but the illumination didn't reach them this deep under the canopy. Facing uphill, he leaned against the rough bark of the trunk and pulled her between his braced legs, his hands cupping her bottom. "Two things," he said, touching his nose to hers. "First—" He kissed her again, this time a tender outpouring of his heart that warmed her to the soles of her feet. "I'm so sorry I scared you, Nat. I never, never meant to."

"I know," she whispered. It should have been a small wound, nothing she couldn't deal with if she had been willing to talk.

"Second, the ménage. We can't even contemplate this without trust and communication. If you aren't ready, say so. At any time. I told him what I told you: I'm not going to have a hand in pressuring you into anything. Shit, I'm not even sure I can handle it." He ran tender fingers along her cheek, and Natalie bent her head into his palm, her throat too full to respond beyond a gruff thank you.

He slid his hands down her back and held her close. "Do you know what he's got in mind?"

"Based on what little he said this morning, I have the gist. Some sort of poly relationship, or a sub-share. God, I sound like an Uber car or something."

Ryan laughed quietly. "Yes and no. Right now, he's proposed more of a mentorship. Mostly it'll be just you and me, since he's way out here. Sometimes we'll all be together. I gather he gets to Seattle on occasion, and if we feel like coming here, this place ain't bad. For the wild." He kissed her on one corner of her mouth. "Sometimes he'll get you to himself." He kissed the opposite corner. "If I don't send a goon squad to tie him up and drop him in that lake," he added under his breath.

"Ryan! Seriously," Natalie said, taking fistfuls of his shirt. "This is part of what I'm worried about. What's to keep you guys from killing each other?"

He took her face between his hands and brushed both thumbs over her cheeks. His eyes were dark, his expression sober. "It's only going to work if we keep the lines of communication open, Nat. You and I have some serious work to do, but it can't be any other way. That means when you're upset, no shutting down, no running away. The same will go for your cowboy and me. You won't be in the middle of that."

She nodded, but in an absent sort of way. Two dominant men. It was one thing to communicate, and another thing entirely to expect they could set aside their natural tendencies and work together in a sexual relationship.

"Hey, Nat," Ryan said, his voice taking on a delectable edge she was already responsive to. "Javier and I will have to work out our side of this. That's partly what tonight's about. If we can get past step one, and if we get through whatever comes next without wounded feelings, we'll all sit down and make sure the ground rules are clear before we move forward. Otherwise, this isn't happening. It's too risky for you. Javier and I agree on that much."

Her nod was more resolute this time, and her heart was growing precariously light. "Okay. Better communication. I promise."

"Perfect." He kissed her again, gentle still, but with a touch more fire. She was breathless when he said, "We should go. Your guy is impatient as all hell. Thinks he's royalty or something."

Natalie chuckled. "He might be. I think there's some *Duque de Granada* history somewhere."

"Well, then, we'd better not keep the bastard waiting." Ryan gathered her hair into a tail with a twist of his wrist and eased down, raising her chin. "Not long, anyway." Then he tossed away whatever restraint he'd been employing. His half-day whiskers scoured her as his lips trailed over her cheeks, down her neck. He spun them around and pinned her hands overhead against the tree, scoring her wrists against the deep-grooved bark of the ponderosa. There was nothing gentle about him now as he palmed her breast, rolled and tugged her nipple the way he knew she loved, nipped her lips, mixing the sharp edges of his teeth with the warm softness of his tongue. A tantalizing promise of life on the uncivilized edge.

Natalie began to reach for the velvety, peaceful blank. Maybe she should have told him Javier never let her do that.

Not long after, Natalie squeezed her eyes closed against the sudden brightness of the porch light illuminating the front of a cabin. The door flew open, and she had a vague sense of herself as a Thanksgiving Day Parade balloon, being towed inside by a string around her ankle.

"Well, I see you've gotten a head start."

Natalie blinked until Javier came into view, sprawled in a wide leather club chair, his brows slashing low over the bridge of his nose.

"I just talked to her," Ryan said. "And kissed her the way I've done a thousand times."

"More than that." Javier's black scowl reached past her shoulder. "You let her start to fly."

"I didn't *let* her do anything. She just...*poof.*"

Javier clicked his tongue, the sound suffused with the kind of disappointment that filled her with a warmth she'd tried to forget. "I suppose we can conclude she's not holding your little stunt with the rent-a-submissive against you any longer," he said, pushing up from his chair. Ryan stayed at her back, warm and solid. "Natalie," Javier said, his familiar rough-skinned fingers rubbing up the underside of her arm.

"I'm right here," she said. He drew the backs of his fingers across her cheek, focusing her attention. She looked into his stern face, watched tense lines evaporate.

"Are you misbehaving, *pequeña*?"

"Maybe." Natalie turned her head. He wouldn't appreciate her amusement. She eased away from the bulwark of Ryan's front.

"Lesson one, *cabrón*. She's far out of practice. I think we can assume she's agreeable to this arrangement for tonight, but even without the prospect of bondage or pain, she's vulnerable. She'll let herself skip to subspace easily enough."

Natalie turned her head, found Ryan in a familiar stance, hands on his hips, looking both annoyed and concerned. "Don't be exasperated, babe," she said. "It's a good thing."

His fingers raked through his hair, and seeing him disconcerted intensified her desire to misbehave in ways certain to earn a swift, decisive response. She had whipsawed from unsure to all-in. Now she wanted nothing more than for Ryan to play out all the fantasies he'd tempted her with, and more.

Javier urged her down into his abandoned chair and squatted at her knees. "I can see your gears turning, *pequeña*. Can I get you something?"

She looked between her men, the rugged one and the polished one. "I'm good," she said, a smile twitching her lips. Nerves layered over enthusiasm, which sat on top of the most carnal of feelings, a sensual onslaught aching in her breasts and between her legs.

Javier crossed the room, reached into a cabinet, and came out with a bottle of Gran Patrón. He poured two glasses and handed one to Ryan. "Have a seat," he said, tilting his glass at the sofa across from the chair. Ryan retreated, and Javier jostled Natalie about until he was sitting beneath her on the chair. She relaxed against him and enjoyed the feel of his calloused fingers rasping over her arm, giving her continual bursts of goose bumps.

"So." Ryan took a hefty swig from his glass, then sat

forward, his elbows on his knees. "What are we doing? You left Nat in the dark. It's time for full disclosure."

There was a heavy pause as Javier absorbed Ryan's accusation. "If there are to be three of us in this relationship, Natalie has to know what to expect from each of us. Consistency will make it easier for all of us. I handle her with strict care, so if you intend to behave in a playful way, it won't work, because, *cabrón*, I am not changing."

Ryan's expression turned mutinous for a brief moment before he replied, "I won't be playful when it matters, I can assure you. But I'm not you. Natalie and I have our own way. These things are negotiated, in my experience, not declared."

"I believe I can speak for myself, boys," Natalie said with her own spike of annoyance, dissipating the last of the lovely haze of her interlude with Ryan. She stared hard, first at him, then at Javier. He dropped a baleful gaze on her. She sat up and pulled the tumbler from his hand, took a careful sip, and then grimaced as the tequila burned down her throat. "Okay, expectations."

"Expectations and consent, *cariño*. Nothing can happen without your consent."

She took a deep breath. "The way I see it, I have no secrets left. You apparently both understand me better than I understand myself."

"That's not consent, though," Javier said. "Consent involves trust, and a willingness to submit to not one, but two doms."

Natalie thought about it for a long moment, but found herself at peace with that aspect of their situation. "Ryan and I will find our way through it, Javier. Like a new couple."

"I agree, but as this is also a mentorship, there must be common rules." His fingers had been exploring places he knew would make her squirm, and now they spidered above her knee, dragging her skirt upward. "He has to be willing to learn, and you have to be willing to be the teaching tool."

She nodded. "I'm willing."

She looked to Ryan, confirming their conversation under the tree. But rather than agreeable, she found him staring fixedly at Javier's fingers playing between her legs, his body tense, as if balanced on a pincushion. For her part, the idea of him watching Javier play with her had the same effect as before. A dark, inexorable pleasure moved inside her like a tide.

Still, Ryan looked to be having second thoughts. "Babe?" Natalie asked softly.

As if she'd bumped him out of a daze, he sat back and took another deep pull of his drink.

In that fraught moment, she knew without a doubt she wanted this. And that she could never choose between them. If their arrangement didn't work, she'd have to say good-bye to them both.

Ryan met her eye. "I'm on board."

Natalie slumped back against Javier's chest. "Relax, *cariño*. It's going to be fine." He nipped the side of her neck and down, to the firm muscle atop her shoulder. She tipped her head and the warmth of his tequila-laced breath washed over her, taking her to old, familiar places as he slipped a finger under the edge of her panties, dipped into her slick heat. "I'll tell you one thing, *cabrón*. Knowing you are watching certainly arouses her."

As did Javier talking about it.

Ryan glanced down, his eyelids half-mast, his expression gone flat, almost disinterested, and yet...not. When he looked back up, Natalie recognized what she had never seen. He was settling into dominant headspace.

Her skin crackled and seethed, sparks running just under the surface. Javier's fingers roamed, and Natalie squirmed under the dueling demands for her attention. Without speaking a word, Ryan delivered a message to her over the rim of his glass—he'd turn the tables soon enough.

She couldn't control her small shiver as the submissive inside her writhed with an itch so deep, Natalie knew scratching it would expose her darkest core. Perhaps she would emerge something closer to her essence, someone who could embrace her nature rather than hide it away. Javier had always encouraged her, and Ryan...well, she was foolish to have slammed the door on him. He spun her out in wholly different ways.

Her alpha side whispered, *Take it. Take it all.*

Javier bolted back his tequila. "Stand up, *pequeña*," he said, his Patrón-scoured voice leaving no room for disobedience. Natalie stood before him on legs like a marionette's, stiff and wooden, yet hinged and unstable. Javier touched a finger to her jaw. "You aren't to take your eyes from me unless I allow you to look away, Natalie. Don't look to him for approval, do you understand?"

The muscles behind her eyes strained as she forced them to stay fixed on him. "Yes, Javier," she whispered. But there remained a sliver of her mind aware of the force pressing on her from behind. Of Ryan's palpable presence.

"Everything off," Javier said.

The simple directive speared through her like a blade, left her hot, liquid, and entirely focused. She toed off her boots and pulled her shirt over her head, her gaze locked on Javier, alert for any signals he might send. He watched her through eyes gone dark as she shimmied out of her skirt and dropped her bra and panties on top.

Javier's gaze trailed over her, tangible as a finger, the lines he drew from point to point buzzing and vibrant on her skin. He put down his glass and beckoned her toward him. "Come closer, *pequeña*."

Natalie stepped between his knees, and he skimmed his

palm over her contour, from her ribs inward along the curve of her waist, out again over her hip, down the length of her thigh. "I call her *mi pequeña* so she knows her place. My little one," he said, ostensibly to Ryan. He drew a figure eight around her breasts, careful to only outline them. "So pale. Do you never get outside anymore?"

"No, Javier." This was how it began, the exquisite stretching of her nerves. He would pull and release until she frayed, until he could snap her with no more than a whisper of touch. Or wind her tighter still.

"My boots, *pequeña*, and my shirt," he said.

She dropped to her knees. How many times had she done this, knelt at his feet to remove his boots? She set each one neatly aside as he required, then stood over him to unbutton his shirt. She pushed it open, exposing his hewn angles and the scars and marks on his burnished skin. She ran her finger over the one she could never leave alone, the silver mark where a brand had accidentally skipped across the right side of his belly. Javier grabbed her wrist and lifted her hand off him. "I didn't tell you that you could touch me, *pequeña*."

Her ears hummed. She hadn't seen Javier deep in dominant mode for more than a year. Nothing he'd done since she'd arrived on the ranch this weekend came close to matching this, but her old associations didn't fail her. She felt her body finding its proper slot as her mind sought the yin to his yang.

He let go of her wrist and jerked his chin, gesturing across the room. "Now his."

Natalie's stomach filled with swirling heat, and she turned to face Ryan, who watched her with a stern expression. She'd never seen his inner Dom come out before, and now she couldn't take her eyes off him. He breathed slowly, his hands dangling limp between his thighs. Javier was wrong about one thing. Ryan had plenty of self-control.

She unlaced his boots and set them aside, then stood and reached for his shirt. But the brittle look in his eye stopped her cold. He reached to caress her breast, perhaps in reassurance, as his gaze moved past her waist. "I'm not sure what the point is."

"She wants to be of help," Javier said from behind her.

After a long pause, Ryan said, "No, I'll leave my shirt on. Kneel down, Natalie. Put your head on the floor, hands next to your knees."

Her full name coming from between his lips gave her pause, but when he looked up, his eyes the hard blue of lapis, she did as she was told.

It felt like several minutes before Ryan shifted above her, before his finger touched the lowest point of her spine. "I haven't seen you like this before," he said, tracing her backbone, knob to knob. "You're the shape of a heart from up here, did you know that?" His hands swept up and out over the contours of her bottom, and then inward to span her waist. "And there's a perfect canvas here for a handprint." He didn't touch her, but she felt the heat of his palm where it hovered over her skin, anticipation making the fine hairs rise all over her body.

Natalie's eyes slid closed. *Please*, she begged in silence as she ground the backs of her wrists into the tight-woven carpet, a physical cue to keep still.

But Ryan shifted again, and the warmth disappeared. Slow footsteps came from behind her, accompanied by the sound of leather hissing through belt loops. "I'd never quite thought of it that way before, but you're right, *cabrón*." Javier sounded deceptively conversational. "From here, I've always seen more of a ripe, juicy pear."

Something brushed between her legs—a finger, or the dangling end of a belt—a bare, maddening touch. Her temperature spiked as she absorbed a wave of need so deep it made her moan. She couldn't stop herself. She inverted her spine, a little dip of invitation.

"Do you see? She is dangerously responsive," Javier said. Ryan grunted in reply. "The inexperienced dominant finds himself a slave to the inflicting of physical pain, to see the evidence of his control. I find the pain originating here far more gratifying," he said, tapping the side of Natalie's head. "To make her ache from what I'm not doing, what I might not do at all. How I might leave her." His belt slithered across her back. "Shining bright with pain, or languid and replete. Or untouched and sobbing with want."

Natalie knew his philosophy by experience, but to have it so baldly stated, to hear the arousal in his voice as he described it…

"But you are not inexperienced, are you," Javier went on. "You discovered this already, I think."

"I admit, I'm not opposed to seeing my handprint go from white to red on a woman's ass," Ryan said, his voice a low, caustic rumble.

Javier chuckled. "Well, there is the inflicting of pain, and the inflicting of pleasure, eh, *cabrón*?" He dropped the belt onto the floor in front of Natalie's face and knelt behind her. His hands stretched along her rib cage and he traced her outline, in at her waist, out with the flare of her hips; the reverse of Ryan's path. The scratch of his fingers left glowing trails across her skin but for where he interrupted them with the soft press of his lips—in the shallow depressions low on her back, then lower, along the crease where her bottom joined her leg.

Natalie breathed in hopeful little pants, but Javier stopped short of her darkest, most intimate places, though his breath drifted over her, torturing her. Without a touch, he drew her taut, and then he grasped her hair.

"Up, *pequeña*." As she sat back on her heels, Javier tucked close behind her. He reached around to grasp her breast, her flesh bulging between his fingers, and she didn't know whose indrawn hiss she heard first, Ryan's or her own. She stared into the unfocused distance as she felt herself begin to climb toward the softness of subspace.

Javier rose onto his knees, taking her with him. His free hand drifted down her body to curve between her legs, where his finger slipped easily through her wet heat. The sound of his gratification thrummed against her back and he pulled her tighter to him, his erection straining under his jeans, fitting along the cleft of her bottom. "Did you wonder why I would ever suggest Ryan and I might share you, *cariño*?"

Natalie's throat was too thick to answer. She could only respond with the smallest shake of her head.

"Stay with me, *pequeña*." His hand grazed up her chest until his fingers pushed against the points of her jaw to raise her chin. "Look at him," he whispered. "Look how he sees you."

Slowly, she focused on Ryan, his heavy, inscrutable stare as he watched her body possessed, witnessed strong hands claiming her. Her arousal spiked hard, a violent beat between her legs.

Javier grunted. "*Si*, she's enjoying this far more than you are, *cabrón*." He slid his hand over her mouth and pulled her head back onto his shoulder." I wonder," he said against her cheek. "Will it please me to see you this way with him, see his hand over your mouth, his fingers deep inside you?"

A moan vibrated in the hollow of her throat as he pressed into her, his thumb drawing up and down, teasing her with near brushes of her clit. So very close. She fought her body to keep her hips from rebelling, from arching into his hand.

"Or will it anger me?" he whispered. "Make me want to snatch you from his arms and fuck you senseless for your effrontery."

Natalie whimpered as her muscles seized around his fingers, a small buzz of orgasmic energy bursting inside her like the grounding of an electrical wire. Just a zap to let off excess voltage.

"Now, now, *pequeña*," he said, the edges of his teeth sliding down her neck, warning her. "You know better."

He circled his thumb around her aching clitoris and curled his fingers inside her, over and over, until she could only breathe in, her lungs burning, oversaturated. "No coming," he reminded her. "Not until I release you."

Fuck that. Fuck this. Everything strained—her back, her hips, the tendons in her thighs. She pushed against Javier's hand and tried to take.

With a suddenness that shocked her, he sat back, jerking her mental tether, depriving her of his heat, of the support of his body. She swayed on her knees, his disappointment washing over her, black as ink. She glanced blearily at Ryan. His deep scowl only added to her apprehension.

"I'm sorry," she whispered.

"When have I ever accepted I'm sorry, *pequeña*?" Javier pulled her arms back. "A reminder, then." He wound his belt around her wrists, bound her tight, and pressed her head back to the floor between Ryan's feet.

A warm, smooth-skinned hand spread between her shoulder blades. "I've never seen you more beautiful," Ryan whispered, his fingers running featherlight down her arm, tracing the edge of the belt, and then sweeping gently over her bottom.

"Are you all right, *pequeña*?" Javier asked.

She nodded, shaking strands of her hair down over her eyes.

"We'll try again, then."

Natalie heard the zip of five buttons freeing in rapid succession as he jerked open his jeans. His fingers dug into her hips hard enough to create a vivid flash, and without warning, he thrust inside her, balls deep, filling her in one uncompromising stroke. "You don't get to make demands, *pequeña*." He punctuated his admonition with another deep plunge that drove her head against the sofa. "You aren't in control. Not with me."

She didn't want to be, not really. She wanted to let Javier propel her up and up, until only he and she existed in the wispy nothingness. But he wouldn't allow it. He drew backward in an excruciating retreat he knew would push her over the edge if he kept it up.

Ryan got in on the game to keep her grounded. He brushed her hair off her face, drew his thumb over her lips. "I'm tempted to make you take my cock in your mouth, Natalie," he said. "So every one of his strokes drives you down my shaft until I can feel the back of your throat closing over me."

She groaned, her imagination fully equal to his, her desire inescapable. Javier hissed in a ragged breath when she clenched around him. He stopped with only his smooth crown of his cock inside her. They hung there, silent and still.

Natalie ground her teeth and kept herself from rocking back and demanding the contact she so desperately craved. Seconds upon seconds of grasping, twitching muscles and silent pleas for relief.

God, Javier was cruel.

And perfect.

Perfectly cruel.

He ran his palms over the roundness of her raised bottom, his thumbs gliding through the cleft between. "I can see why you'd want her to, *cabrón*." Slowly, Javier eased himself deep inside her. "I will never tire of the sight of my cock disappearing between her lips." He pulled back just as slowly, and then, gradually, with the precision of years of experience, his pace accelerated.

He drove through her, sleek and absolute, forcing low cries from her, desperation given voice. She wanted to scream with the depth of her need, with the pain of staving off her orgasm, and its pleasure. But those same clashing ecstasies kept her attentive to her submissive side. If she lost control, it would all be for naught. He'd leave her naked and destitute.

And so she bit her lip and tried to find the elusive mastery of her body, all while Javier ground out how he would have used her had she remained his, how he would use her once again, as he uttered vulgar Spanish curses that made her want to be and do all the things he spoke of. He fanned the fire inside her, scorched her from the inside out.

"Oh fuck," she breathed.

"Hey," Ryan snapped, his voice cutting through her fog. "Hold up, cowboy."

Javier halted and pulled suddenly free of her. "*Hostias, cariño*," he said, stretching on the carpet alongside her, careful not to touch her anywhere with more than a gentle finger. "Look at me. What happened to your safe word?"

"Don't stop," she said. "Please don't."

"You're crying, Natalie," Javier said. "You're too far out of practice, even for this nothing." He pushed another loose strand of hair out of her eyes.

His face, stern and loving, drifted in and out as she blinked slowly. "It's so good," she said. "I forgot."

Ryan groaned above her, and she uttered a breathy laugh. She'd heard that exasperated sound so many times. "I know, babe," she said. "What can I say? I like the torture."

Javier reached between her legs and she inched them apart. "I want nothing more than to torture you, *pequeña*." His fingers played over her in slow, luxurious swirls. "But I think we should stop."

"No!" Natalie begged. "Please, Javier. This might be my

only chance."

"Don't fret, *cariño*. There's always another time."

She blinked at him, stunned. He wouldn't leave her like this. "You can't."

One corner of his mouth twitched. Games. He was messing with her.

"Oh, you fucking sadist," she slurred.

Without removing his hand, Javier rose and shifted behind her. He slid deep inside her, gentle at first, then hard and fast, with no let-up this time. Natalie gasped and panted through parted lips as he used her, thrilled her, and finally, graciously, allowed her climax to engulf her.

Her body was limp, but her heart still beat a thunderous rhythm when Javier gave her the closest he would ever come to a playful swat and said, "No rest, *pequeña*."

"What?" she gasped.

He touched a finger to the thudding vein in her neck. "I let you take your pleasure. Now it's our turn, or have you forgotten how this goes?"

Natalie stared into his deep green eyes and admitted nothing.

"You squandered more than a year with me, and for months you played a cruel game with Ryan. You owe each of us restitution."

Natalie's blood surged through her veins. "I should have known," she said under her breath.

"You should have," he agreed. "Nothing comes free, *cariño*. And your Ryan still has plans tonight."

In a split second, as if she were little more than a roped calf, Javier had her ass up, face down over Ryan's thighs. "Give him your safe word."

"Estepona," she said automatically, even though she hadn't spoken it in over a year.

"Estepona," Ryan said, wrapping his mouth around the

Spanish word. "Good thing we won't need it." He circled his palm across the entire surface of her backside, at once soothing and nerve-racking. "Only five, Nat. Since I was partly to blame."

She nodded as anxiety-coated desire unspooled inside her. She'd never let anyone other than Javier strike her.

"Add five for me, *cabrón*," Javier said. "For insulting me. I'm no sadist."

"Fine. Ten, then. You count, Natalie," Ryan said. "And no complaints. I owe you twice as many for getting off on making me watch you two the last couple of days, so consider yourself lucky. And try not to scream your throat raw. I have plans for it after this."

Natalie said, "Yes, Ryan," and Javier ruffled his fingers through her hair.

"This might just work out well, *cariño*. I like your Ryan. I think the three of us will do fine." He sat down across from them, his hand idly tracing up and down his cock as it hardened once again.

Ryan anchored his hand across her lower back, and Javier offered him a small nod. Natalie turned and looked hard over her other shoulder as Ryan raised his hand. "Almost like my limo fantasy. What do you say?"

A small, gratified smile tugged at her lips.

"Please, Ryan."

Natalie opened her eyes to a shaft of bright sunlight spearing across the ceiling. It took her two blinks to work out where she was, and a slow grind of her brain to identify all the parts that surrounded her. Javier's back to her front, and Ryan's hips against her butt, his thigh tucked up against hers from behind, someone's fingers tracing over her hip.

"We left marks," Ryan whispered.

She glanced down. "It's okay. No one besides us will see them."

"I never bruised you before."

Natalie couldn't be sure if it was wonder or sadness she heard in his voice. She put her hand atop his. "No, you didn't. You were always careful of me. But this isn't you being careless."

He hummed, accepting her response, she hoped, and settled closer against her back.

The sun was up, and Javier shouldn't still be in bed, but here he was. The thought that they were all still lying there like a pile of puppies brought a smile to Natalie's face. How was it possible she'd fallen in love with two men who would willingly share her?

Ryan's fingers twitched again on her leg. "What's so funny?" Natalie craned her neck to look over her shoulder, and when she did, Ryan captured her lips with his before she could answer. "Morning, babe," he said.

He scooted back enough to allow Natalie room to turn onto her back, gently, so as not to wake Javier. "You aren't feeling smug, are you?" she asked.

"Maybe a little." He pressed his forehead against her temple. "I missed you so fucking much."

Tears pricked her eyes. She had missed him, too, even though she'd spent so much of their time apart convincing herself he was the villain. "I'm so sorry, Ryan."

"No, babe, don't." He caught the rogue tear that escaped from the corner of her eye with his lips, just before it made it to her ear. "I didn't mean to make you cry."

"It's an angry tear—anger at myself. I'm allowed one."

His finger traced her features—the curve of her eyebrow, the ridge of her cheekbone, the end of her nose. "Fine. One. But that's all. We're starting over. All of us."

His words brought back a question Natalie had thought about deep in the night, but hadn't had the nerve to ask. She turned again, this time to face him. "You aren't bothered when Javier and I…"

His face took on a comical air of expectation. "When you…? Say it, Natalie. You know I love it when you talk dirty."

"Ass." Natalie gave him a light shove to the chest.

He pressed his hand atop hers, holding her palm over his heartbeat, his expression serious. "Yesterday, after I met with Javier, I did a little research. I didn't want to react in a way that would freak you out. I needed to know what to expect, and to be prepared. I kept seeing this term, *compersion*."

Natalie shook her head. "Never heard of it."

"Me, either. Everywhere I looked described it the same way: the flip side of jealousy. The feeling of being genuinely happy seeing your lover enjoy another lover."

"Huh. So, is that how you reacted?"

Ryan sniffed. "Not exactly. Not fully. But it was remarkable how much I enjoyed watching him take you into deeper submission as the night went on. Granted, I probably would have enjoyed it more if I'd gotten you there, but as far as second places go, it wasn't terrible."

"So glad to have entertained you," Natalie replied, smiling as his hand smoothed over her bottom. There had to be significant marks there, too. And on her thighs, and…well, a lot of places.

"You were beautiful, and your enjoyment was beautiful. There were moments I wanted to yank you away, but…" His gaze turned inward. "I'm surprised by the emotions it spurred. And what it didn't spur."

"So, you don't want to kill Javier?"

"I didn't say that, did I?"

"Can you two *hijos de las gran putas* save this conversation for when someone isn't trying to sleep?" Javier's voice, so annoyed and gruff, even muffled by his pillow, made both Natalie and Ryan grin.

"What did he say?" Ryan asked.

"He called us sons of big bitches. He's mad," Natalie mock-whispered in reply.

Ryan snorted a laugh, and Javier made a show of putting a pillow over his head.

Natalie pulled her lips between her teeth. When she composed herself, she picked up the corner of the pillow. "Sorry, *mi sol*," she told Javier. "Aren't you supposed to be at the barns?"

"No," he said, with a regal air. How he did it in one word, Natalie had never figured out. "I made arrangements with the foreman, and now they are wasted."

Natalie turned over and pressed her body against Javier's. "Aw, now who's the grumpy one?" She spooned her legs with his and reached around his hip, not the least surprised to find him hard, although after last night, he could be excused for being worn out.

She closed her fingers around him and dragged upward, then adjusted her hold to include his balls. His rumble of pleasure vibrated through his back, joined by Natalie's "Oh!" as, from behind, Ryan drew a finger through her exposed flesh, finding her wet, if a bit tender. He fitted against her, his cock between her legs, smoothing across her with slow, gentle strokes. Strokes she matched with her hand on Javier's cock. And when Ryan pushed inside her, she squeezed Javier tighter, her hand moving up and down with ever more purpose.

It was an interesting ballet, the three of them. In the silence of morning, Natalie was exquisitely aware of every small noise, and every more substantial one. Grunts and sighs, Ryan speaking in English behind her, Javier in Spanish in front her, the sounds her body made as Ryan filled her and retreated. Nothing above a whisper, just the softness of the three of them moving as one, languid and fluid, until Ryan's fingers tightened on her hip, and Natalie used the back of Javier's thigh to stimulate her clit, his hand closing over hers, the blur of motion as they worked together. Their climaxes broke over them, somehow nearly synchronous, and, in the way of early morning sex, sleepily. Less sound and fury, more soft solemnity.

As they lay in each other's arms after, Natalie nestled in a cocoon of warm skin and cotton sheets, she couldn't think of any place she'd rather be. For too long she'd buried her true self, and now she ached to be free.

"We're doing this, right?" she said. "Not just last night, but again."

"Maybe," Ryan said.

"No," Javier stated.

Natalie's eyes flew open, and Ryan raised his head, both of them looking in Javier's direction, neither of them seeming to breathe. His eyes remained peacefully closed, but the corners of his lips twitched in a terrible, devious hint of a smile. "Next time Ryan gets the hand job. I want to be buried inside you."

"Oh, you wretch," Natalie said, but she didn't have the energy to state it as forcefully as she'd have liked. There was a small *poof* behind her as Ryan's head hit the pillow.

"It's up to you, *cariño*," Javier said, patting her thigh. "Remember? That's the point."

Behind her, Ryan's breaths deepened and grew slower, and before long, Javier's did as well. Natalie already knew her decision, and knowing these men, they did, too. Still, if she'd learned one thing yesterday, it was that they would want her to affirm it.

She turned her head one way, and then the other, before giving a quiet, *pfft*. Kind of hard to affirm a damn thing when they were both asleep. Natalie nestled more comfortably between them and closed her eyes, too, just for a minute.

When she opened them again, light poured in from everywhere, the scent of bacon wafted into the bedroom, and sounds of clattering dishes let her know Ryan was on breakfast duty. God knows, she'd never seen Javier cook anywhere but over a campfire. Natalie sat up and stretched, then flopped back down, and spread her arms and legs, reveling in the fact that she had the entire bed to herself.

Ryan appeared in the doorway, a spatula in hand. "Finally. Come on, Ms. Starfish. I'm starving, and Javier has to leave."

Natalie's stomach rumbled. "Is there coffee? I don't smell coffee."

"Of course there's coffee. Do you think we don't know your morning needs?"

Natalie raised her head and offered him a sultry smile. "No, you're both very knowledgeable."

"That's right. Now up, before I have to spank you to make you get out of bed." She opened her mouth to protest that was no way to entice her out, but Ryan held up a finger. "I am in control of the coffee."

"Fine." Natalie struggled upright, then found one of the robes provided by the ranch for the use of guests, and padded out to the kitchen.

Ryan had put on his jeans, but he was still shirtless. Natalie took a moment to stare at his smoothly muscled back and shoulders as he worked at the stove, until Javier, fully dressed, boots and all, stepped between her and her view. He tugged her close with the belt of her robe.

"Damn," Natalie said, spearing her hands into his rear pockets. He smelled freshly showered, and his beard had been trimmed sharp. "You have to go?"

"I hate to lose you when I've just gotten you back, *cariño*."

Natalie kissed him on the chin. "I squandered your free morning by sleeping."

"Not quite all of it," Javier replied with the sort of look on his face that gave Natalie an intense rush of warmth. There were few things as wonderful as knowing she could bring a man like Javier to his knees.

"I'll see you when you all leave the ranch," he went on. "But I won't be able to give you a proper good-bye." He gave her a tender kiss. "Or tell you next weekend will be much more of a challenge, so be prepared."

"Next weekend?"

"I thought I'd come to the big city. Assuming you want to keep exploring this." He circled his finger to include all three of them.

Natalie turned to look at Ryan, who stood with his arms crossed. He looked simultaneously forbidding and worried, prepared for the worst. She rose on her toes to kiss Javier on the lips, then spoke to them both. "I do. I could never choose between you. It's all or nothing for me." She glanced again at Ryan and held his gaze as she said, "I've tried nothing. It wasn't great."

Javier patted her bottom. "I'm gratified to hear you say so, *pequeña*. I expect you to behave." He gave a resolute nod over her head, including Ryan in his pronouncement. "*Te amo, mi amor*," he whispered against her lips.

Ryan made a loud *tsk*ing sound behind her. "Always showing off with the Spanish."

"You have to admit, *cabrón*, it does sound better." Javier settled his hat on his head and turned for the cabin's front door.

Natalie grinned. Ryan brought out something playful in Javier, while Javier bolstered Ryan's dominant side, but between the three of them, there was no doubt. She was the winner.

As they watched Javier stride downhill, Ryan kissed her favorite spot near her ear. "I love you, too."

Natalie turned into his arms. "I still owe you. Both of you."

"Nope," he said, distracting her with a kiss. "No more looking backward."

She didn't challenge him. After all, he was in control. If he ever wanted to collect, she'd be ready. He was right. Now it was time to look forward, plan ahead—all three of them. They would have all the time they needed.

Acknowledgments

Putting the story-words on the page (or screen) may seem like a one-person endeavor, but getting those words ready for prime time is absolutely a group effort. All the love to my husband and family, who kept me grounded and caffeinated, and to my writer's group and critique partners, who kept me laughing, boosted my ego, and let me know when this story threatened to fly off the rails. To Nicole, Margaret, and Toria, especially, first readers (and first fans), so much gratitude. And to the others in my crazy gang, all of whom took part in making Natalie's story better, my humblest thanks.

To those at Entangled, especially my editor, Brenda, publicists Holly and Riki, and Curtis in production, thank you for putting up with a lot of rookie questions, and for answering them all with patience and grace. You've made this a smooth ride.

About the Author

Renee Dominick lives and works in the Seattle suburbs, a place perfectly suited to her love of all things nature, and for writing atmospheric and steamy erotic romance.

When she's not melded to her laptop, she's probably reading, watching off-beat movies, poking around in her garden (assisted by her two terriers,) or planning her next big adventure.

Her super-sexy short story, *Through Glass a Stranger*, can be found in the erotic anthology, *kINKED*. Visit her website at ReneeDominick.com, and find her on Twitter @Renee_Dominick.

If you love erotica, one-click these hot Scorched releases...

Big Catch
a *Dossier* novella by Cathryn Fox

Former New York stockbroker, Brayden Adams takes one look at Alyssa and knows she needs to relax. He'd known the feeling himself, until he and his best friend, Tyler, left the fast life behind when they inherited a hotel and fishing business in Antiqua. Now they live a relaxed island life and share everything. But Alyssa makes him question everything he knows.

Loving Her Alphas
a novel by Ari Thatcher

After a wolf attacks Rayne Adler near her grandfather's lodge, the Whitmore brothers nurse her back to health. Unaware they are wolf-shifters, she finds each appealing in a different way. But, she's not at Shady Pines Lodge for romance, nor would she ever choose between them. The successful businesswoman is there only to refurbish the grounds and bring tourism back to the area. Caleb, Nick, and Dalton are thrilled to finally have found their mate in spunky Rayne Adler and will use everything in their power to persuade her that she was made for them. All three of them.

Two Dukes and a Lady
a novel by Lorna James

Dukes Charles Ashdown and William Kenwood love womanizing too much to ever be ensnared by a debutante. Certainly, no decent wife would allow their debauchery. But the only woman they've ever loved is back. After her husband's mysterious death, Lillian Drew finds solace with her girlhood crushes, Charles and William. When her dead husband's creditors hound her, she has no choice but to remarry, though she can't make up her mind which duke she'll propose to.

Ruthless
a *Playboys in Love* novel by Gina L. Maxwell

People call me Ruthless for a reason. Whether I'm in the court room or in the bedroom, my reputation is well-earned. I'm either working hard, working out, or working my way into some woman's panties. But none of them share my particular kink, and I walk away feeling unsatisfied. Until I met *her*.